John Finbow, a successful writer, and his wife Kay move into Southcombe Rectory, a large Victorian house that has been empty since the 1960s. It had previously been owned by the Cuthbertson family who had lived there for generations. Their marriage is under strain, as John, 39 would like children before he gets too old, but Kay, 34, does not.

When John is working in his study soon after moving in, he is disturbed by the sight of a young woman who appears out of the blue on his sofa. Emily Cuthbertson, whose old bedroom is now John's study, was 25 at the time of her death and the youngest of 8 offspring of the late Reverend Arthur Cuthbertson and his wife Delia. Emily had died in 1868 but is now unwilling to leave behind her old life on earth, due to having missed out on a family of her own whilst being a companion to her widowed mother. Emily is still desperate for a husband and children, and John is the answer to her dreams.

One hundred and thirty years separate them. Will Emily and John's love survive time's relentless march?

PARTNERS IN TIME

A novel by
STEVIE TURNER

ACKNOWLEDGEMENTS

Thanks to Laura at LLPix Designs (http://llpix.com) for the cover.

CONTENTS

PART 1
FEBRUARY 1867

CHAPTER 1 – EMILY

There's ice on the inside of the windows again. Peggy needs to re-light the fires; it's six thirty and she should have been up by now.

Emily Cuthbertson drew the ribbon of her nightshirt a little tighter around her neck and burrowed underneath the counterpane, sighing with relief when she heard the welcome light tap on the door.

"Come in!"

Peggy, more red-faced and flustered than usual, carried a full scuttle of coal and kindling, and headed straight for a mound of white ash in the fireplace, scraping out the grate with practised ease. Kindling in place, she struck a Lucifer match and turned to Emily.

"Sorry I'm a bit late, Miss Emily."

It had been her father, the formidable Reverend Cuthbertson, who had always dealt with recalcitrant servants. But the reverend was no more, and with her mother still prostrate in her room next door with grief, Emily sat up and realised it would probably always now fall to her to keep the staff on their toes.

"Don't let it happen again, Peggy."

"No, Miss. I'll just go and get your hot water."

Emily waited until Peggy had left the room, and then sank back on the pillows. Her life was not panning out exactly as she had hoped. She was twenty five, and as far as she was concerned, although the youngest in the family she was already quite the old maid. One by one her seven siblings had married and moved away or abroad, ensuring they were not the last one left at home and thereby duty bound to provide companionship to their ailing mother. Emily felt a frisson of discontent; the chance to marry and have children of her own was passing her by. Her 64 year old mother could live for another ten or twenty years at least, by then her own youthful bloom would have all but evaporated in the ravages of time.

A knock on her door signalled the arrival of the hot water jug. Another miserable day's existence loomed, and she could do nothing about it.

***

"How can I eat breakfast, Emily?" Delia Cuthbertson, pale and wan, sat propped up against a mountain of pillows and pushed away her tray. "Your father is dead."

Emily gently nudged it back towards the widow.

"It's been three months now. Papa wouldn't have wanted you to stop eating."

"I want to join him." Delia's eyes filled with tears. "There's no point in going on."

With one uncharacteristic angry sweep of Delia's arm, a plate of hot porridge sailed through the air and landed on the floor, accompanied by uncontrollable weeping. Emily sighed as she looked at the glutinous mess on the rug.

"I'll go and find Peggy."

The maid was busy sweeping dust from the entrance hall floor out into the garden. Emily enjoyed a brief flashback as she recalled stepping carefully in each diamond-shaped tile as a child to avoid the cracks. When she emerged from her reverie she noticed a man clothed in strange attire, looking over his shoulder at her as he walked out of the front door into the snow.

"Porridge has been spilled onto the rug in Mrs Delia's room."

"I'll see to it straight away, Miss." Peggy put her broom to one side. "Shall I take the tray away?"

Emily nodded and took a glimpse outside.

"Yes, I think so. Peggy…who is that person you've been speaking to? Is he a tradesman?"

She turned back towards the hallway when she received no reply, but Peggy had already disappeared upstairs. Emily, puzzled as to the man's identity, walked out onto the lawn, but the man had seemingly vanished into thin air.

Her mother's sobbing had reached a zenith in front of a captive audience by the time Emily returned. Peggy stoically scrubbed the rag rug but remained silent while Emily decided to pour some tea into a cup and place it in Delia's shaking hand.

"Drink this. It'll make you feel better."

Platitudes that she was certain would fall on deaf ears, but she needed to say something to try and lighten the atmosphere. The spinning vortex of misery threatening to devour them all needed to be stopped in its tracks. Delia took a sip and gazed sightlessly at her daughter, her mind in a state of turmoil.

"I'm so alone!"

"Nonsense." Emily plumped up the pillows behind her mother's back. "You have eight grown up children. How can you be alone?"

"But I only see *you*."

Emily was tired of the same conversation going around and around but reaching no satisfactory conclusion.

"Because you won't get out of bed and visit them! They all have busy lives. Mama, you read Lionel's letter last week - he'll be moving back soon to take over father's duties, so at least you'll see *him* every day."

There was no reply from her mother. Emily sighed, and for the thousandth time wished her father was still around.

CHAPTER 2

Days followed the same routine in that she would draw and paint as a means of escape, but also try to be the good companion that her mother needed her to be. With the arrival of her clergyman brother Lionel bringing an end to the interregnum and with Emily's cajoling and encouragement, her mother Delia had started to raise herself out of bed. With life on a more even keel, Emily decided the time was right to offer a suggestion as she brushed her mother's long silver hair one spring morning in March.

"It would be nice if Beatrice and Alfred could stay for a weekend with the baby. I think I'll write to them. I know you miss Beattie as much as I do."

She took some pins from her mother's hand and twirled a long ringlet around her finger before affixing it next to the others. When the reply came, a small wave of excitement coursed through her body.

"That would be a good idea, I think. Little Amelia must be nearly two years old now."

Emily could hardly wait to get to the task. When Delia was suitably dressed and engrossed in *The Times*, she opened her father's bureau and selected some notepaper and a matching envelope. As she wrote she imagined with envy her eldest sister ensconced in marital bliss in Lamburn, only six miles from Southcombe as the crow flew, but now a busy mother and wife to Lamburn's only watch and clockmaker.

With the letter written, she buttoned her boots and fastened her cape securely. It was time to enjoy some fresh air and take a walk to post the invitation. Across the green she spied Lionel, who waved to her as he pinned a notice in the entrance to the church. Miss Routledge cycled towards the schoolroom, where several children were already chasing each other in the playground. Emily walked briskly past the school she had attended for 9 years and came to a halt outside the post office. A bell above the door tinkled softly as she entered. She smiled at the postmistress and inhaled the familiar sweet aroma of her favourite crystallised fruits and aniseed balls.

"Good morning, Mrs Edgecombe."

Lucy Edgecombe, large and motherly, returned the smile with one of her own.

"It's a fine morning, Miss Emily."

Emily placed her addressed envelope on the counter.

"Indeed it is. I need a stamp please, if you would be so kind."

She handed over a penny as the postmistress scrutinised the envelope.

"I haven't seen Miss Beatrice for some years."

Emily ignored a stab of irritation and decided to be as affable and charming as Lionel.

"Mama would like them all to pay a visit."

"I hope she comes to see me if she does." Lucy took the penny and affixed a stamp to the envelope. I'll pop this in the sack for you."

"Thank you." Emily gave a little nod. "Good day for now."

She wanted her burst of freedom to last a while longer. It had been quite some time since she had been inside a church, and Lionel had always been her favourite brother.

There was a cool essence of musk or suchlike as she opened the church's heavy oak door. A serene stillness had settled over the pews, their ends still draped in cream organza ribbons from a recent wedding. Emily walked slowly up the aisle, wondering whether one day she might undertake the same walk as a radiant bride. Lionel was seated in the vestry, scribbling frantically in a notebook.

"Emily! How good it is to see you here!" He stood up. "I was just finishing Sunday's sermon."

She shrugged.

"I don't know why I came in really. Perhaps I'm getting religious after all these years."

"Each in his own time." Lionel smiled. "I've always had hope that you'd turn to God eventually."

Emily shook her head.

"Don't bet on it. God doesn't seem to like me much, I think. Perhaps it's because I don't go to church every Sunday?"

She wanted to hug her brother. He was so earnest and sure that somewhere just out of sight his God was beaming down benignly.

"God loves you, Emily. He has a plan for you. You just have to find Him when you're ready."

"Yes, my plan is obviously to listen to Mama complaining for the rest of my life." Emily laughed, but inside she felt like crying. "Like I said, your God doesn't seem to be doing *me* many favours."

She did not turn away as Lionel took her hand in his.

"Your chance will come when you least expect it. You know my friend Wilkie – I've told him about your paintings. He's writing a book that needs some illustrations."

Affecting a shrill laugh, Emily let go of her brother's hand and walked towards the vestry door.

"Don't get carried away with your God and be late for dinner. It'll make Mama cross."

"Look for Him." Lionel gave her a small wave. "And you will find Him."

She thought of his words that night as she donned her nightshirt and got into bed. As she closed her eyes, she wondered where Lionel's supposed God of Love was hiding.

CHAPTER 3 – JOHN
JULY 1996

So this is what it's like to be successful …

John Finbow, an enigmatic smile lifting the corners of his mouth, kicked up the stand and swung a leg over the seat of his motorbike, walking it back carefully over the gravel for a few more feet in order to admire his new purchase one more time.

The old south-facing Victorian rectory gazed back at him myopically through sixteen sun-drenched sightless windows framed in drooping wisteria. Ornate chimneys which had survived 170 years of coal fires now stood redundant atop a renewed roof of Welsh slate. A couple of blackened boot scrapers stood symmetrically either side of four grand pillars guarding an entrance portal made of oak, worthy of one of those historical costume dramas that he knew Kay was so fond of.

He could see the previous owner's gardener, Max, already hard at work training stray fronds of peach, apple and pear along the boundary walls, but the jungle of grass hadn't yet been cut to a respectable length. John, beginning to sweat in his leathers, let his mind dwell on his as yet unborn child as *he*, it would have to be a *he*, pedalled a red tricycle on the front lawn.

He emerged from his reverie, and took a deep sigh of happiness as he kick-started the bike. He returned Max's farewell wave with one of his own, and rode gingerly over the gravel until he reached the open iron gates leading out onto Church Lane. Yes, purchasing Southcombe Rectory was a sure sign that he had come up in the world.

***

He spied her amidst a pile of packing crates in the kitchen, one strand of red hair had escaped from her ponytail and flopped over her forehead as she carefully wrapped glassware in yesterday's news. John let a wave of tenderness engulf him as he snuggled up to Kay's back and wrapped his arms about her slim waist.

"My helmet's full of flies."

A snort of laughter escaped from her lips.

"You can get some cream for that, can't you?"

"Nah, just a bit of a lick and a polish."

"Ugh." Kay reached down and behind, gently squeezing his testicles. "You're gross."

He pressed his nose into the warmth of her neck, loving her more than he could ever say. He owed her everything. It had been Kay, who without his knowledge had taken that rejected screenplay from the outside bin where he had thrown it in disgust. The rest, as they say, was history.

"The deal's complete now; we can move in anytime."

She turned to face him, green eyes ablaze, and slid her arms around his neck.

"I told you you'd make it in the end. You should've had more faith in yourself."

"What colour shall we paint the nursery?" He kissed the top of her head. "You know what they say - new house, new baby."

Kay shook her head.

"Not yet. Give me time to get used to being Mrs Finbow first; especially the Mrs Finbow who wears slinky designer dresses and gets invited to film premieres."

He tried to keep his disappointment hidden.

"Okay, but let's not leave it too long, eh? We're not getting any younger."

"Speak for yourself!" Kay thumped him on the chest. "I'm only thirty four!"

"And I'm nearly forty" John sighed. "Some people are grandparents by then." He lifted up a strand of dark brown hair. "I'm already going a bit grey, for Pete's sake."

She disentangled her arms, and without replying turned back rather too quickly to the packing, and John knew he had pushed the issue a little too far. However, his wife's reluctance to give up her PA post to that Timothy Burns-Williams twat and become a mother was somehow unsettling; *didn't all women want babies?*

***

For the first time in his life he did not have to worry about receiving the removal company's invoice, although he mused on whether they had counted up the number of bedrooms and added on another thousand pounds. Money was dripping through his fingers like water, but with every subsequent TV series he wrote, copious amounts of fifty pound notes were appearing on the tree for picking. He was on a roll, and life was good. He knew it would be even better when Kay decided to stop taking that little pill …

His footsteps echoed on bare floorboards that second morning after Kay had left for work in the nearby village of Brackenrye. He knew he should be packing up boxes or settling down to write, but he could almost hear the house demanding that he visit each room to introduce himself before they moved in for good.

John decided to start on the large open-plan fourth floor level. He assumed part of it had once been a nursery and schoolroom, as there were remnants of a worm-infested gate guarding past generations from tumbling base over apex down the main staircase. He'd noticed a succession of Victorian and Edwardian clergymen on the deeds, and imagined them in the bosom of their families, each one with a wife and at least ten children apiece. The nursery was empty, but the bedrooms for a nanny and governess still had some old carpet down and ghastly flock wallpaper, some of it peeling in long strips where perhaps a child from long ago had decided that they didn't like it either.

The children's bathroom next to the nursery looked as though it had not been updated since the 1950s at least, and John couldn't wait to get the decorating team in. His babies' nursery would be state-of-the-art, with enough painted murals and hanging mobiles to hopefully augment their already higher than average IQ. No governess for them, as only Eton or Harrow would do.

He watched a finger of sunshine illuminate some dust motes in his line of vision before descending to the third floor, noticing as he did so some lighter squares and rectangles on the striped wallpaper where perhaps children's paintings had hung. Eight empty bedrooms and three bathrooms led off from a galleried landing. He opened the doors and peeped into each one, hardly able to believe that his own creative talents had led him so far away from the council estates he and Kay had grown up on and from where their parents had been so determined to spend their last days.

He looked over the balcony towards their own bedroom and en-suite bathroom sequestered away on a kind of mezzanine floor below, next to his study. He gave a wry smile, knowing he would be running up and down the stairs every night to check on his eight children whilst Kay slept the sleep of the unconcerned.

Walking around the ground floor level he basked in the sight of four spacious reception rooms, each one with panoramic views of the extensive grounds. He let his eyes travel over the kitchen, dining room, cloakroom and conservatory, and finally the large entrance hall complete with original black and white tiles, swiftly coming to the conclusion that the house needed children, many children, to fill it. He took one last glimpse over his shoulder before strolling contentedly out of the door.

CHAPTER 4 - KAY

She could not quell the butterfly feeling in her stomach as she stood in the hallway of their ground floor maisonette where they had laughed and loved. Kay could hear the removal lorry pulling up outside; John was already shouting out how there was plenty of room to park, but a shadow of despair had crept over her at the thought of leaving behind all that was familiar.

How could a girl become the lady of the manor if she was just plain Kay Lewis from the Broadberry council estate? Who the hell would ever take her seriously?

Kay traced a finger along the rag-roll effect wallpaper that she and John had chosen together, an excited couple starting out in wedded bliss just eighteen months' previously. She had married an archivist at the Broadberry museum who wrote novels and plays in his spare time, but now, because of her own stupid actions, she was the wife of an internationally recognised screenwriter. Life was hurtling along too fast; she wanted to stay in her comfort zone, but knew John was hell-bent on living his dream of winning every literary prize going and filling up their mansion with babies and bikes. It wasn't what she had signed up for; she just wanted a quiet life.

The front door burst open, and his smile lit up her heart.

"They're here! Time to get cracking!"

Kay stifled a sob as she watched him fasten the straps of his crash helmet.

"Okay." She raised a shaky thumb. "Let's be off to Finbow Palace. Good thing Tim's given me the week off. I'll drop the key off at the estate agent's on the way."

She took one last look at her home that now belonged to somebody else, before locking the door and climbing into her car amongst the breakables, photo albums, and precious trinkets. Ensuring the John and his bike were well out of sight, she let a few tears fall as she watched the removal van pull away with all her earthly possessions.

*****

The iron gates stood open to the elements as Kay turned the wheel left onto the gravel, noticing that John had already parked his bike next to the removal van and was busy ferrying furniture into the house. The age-old portals felt warm in the summer sun as she brushed past, impatient to begin unpacking. John gave her a wink.

"I've boiled the kettle, but I can't find any cups."

"I've got them in the boot, and the coffee. No milk though." She replied with a shaky smile.

"Great." John placed a heavy box down with a grunt. "Anything'll do, I'm parched."

Kay turned around, skirting past the removal men, and blinked against the waves of heat shimmering above the car's roof. She lifted a box of mugs from the boot and glanced up at the front of the house, shivering inwardly at the thought of numerous creepy-crawlies and earwigs that might be scooting about amongst the wisteria, boring their way through the old windowsills and into the house. She made a mental note to get John to ask the gardener to chop away fronds from every glass pane.

Everything in the kitchen was strange to her, except the mugs with their yellow smiley faces. The ancient water pipes rattled when she turned on the taps, echoing somewhat in a room three times as big to what she'd been used to. She looked up at the high and ornate plastered ceiling to the cobwebs which festooned every corner, and her heart sank a few more degrees into a looming depression.

Why on earth hadn't she stopped him going through with the purchase? He had been so set on buying the monstrosity of a house that she hadn't had the heart to dissuade him. Now she was stuck with it!

***

Even walking from the en-suite to the bed caused many floorboards to groan in protest. Kay, naked, flopped down onto the mattress and threw off the sheet.

"God, it's hot tonight." She moved her thick auburn hair away from the back of her neck. "Let's make re-building the bed the first job tomorrow, so we're not sleeping on the floor."

She rolled over on her back and closed her eyes, aware of the heat from her husband's body as he moved on top of her.

"What about christening the bedroom then?"

"Aren't you knackered with all that humping?" She laughed and clasped her arms and legs around his back.

"No. I want to do some more, just a different sort."

Slowly and with increasing pleasure, she moved into a familiar rhythm with him on her favourite blue sheet trimmed with violets, which still bore the fragrance of sunlight and fresh air from their old garden which she had loved so much.

CHAPTER 5

It had taken a few weeks, but Kay was beginning to feel at home in the old rectory, especially after a team of cleaners had set to work and removed acres of cobwebs and ground-in dirt of centuries. With money no problem she decided to advertise for an interior designer to bring the rooms around to the 21st century. Within a short time she had willing designers virtually queueing up along the driveway in their earnest efforts to create aesthetically pleasing transformations, and her evenings were increasingly spent poring over portfolios.

"How's it going with the painters and decorators?"

She looked around absent-mindedly as John sunk down into the sofa beside her.

"My period finished today."

"No, not that!" He laughed. "Have you found a designer that's not going to bleed us dry?"

"Not yet." She shook her head and passed him a book of samples. "But this one here looks good. I love this fabric-type wallpaper."

"Wallpaper's retro. Plastered walls look better."

"But look how well it goes with the curtains." She kissed his cheek. "Go on, you know I'm right."

"Just as long as I get to say what goes in my study."

She nodded.

"Okay. Your *man-cave*, you mean?"

"Whatever". He laughed. "Yeah, my man-cave." He flicked through and pointed to a Seventies' type leaf effect. "I can't write if I've got to look at *that* ghastly wallpaper all day. I think the word here would be *noisome*."

"You're so full of sh.. I mean, *words*. Okay, I think I'll go with old Percy then". Kay plumped a large portfolio in John's lap. "Have a look at this one. Percival Ye Myint's an unusual-looking chap from un-exotic Hackney Wick. He's got some great ideas."

She could see acute boredom etched on his features as he idly thumbed through the pages.

"Yeah, it's better than the last one." He yawned. "Whatever…"

She snuggled up to him.

"We're so lucky, aren't we?"

"And it's all down to you." He kissed the top of her head. "There's just one more thing that would make my life complete."

She stiffened in the knowledge of what was to come.

"I told you, John, I'm not ready for motherhood. In fact I'm not sure if I'll ever be."

The silence was awkward between them. When she eventually spoke again, she hated the sound of her thin, reedy voice.

"I'm sorry. I know it's not what I first told you and hey, it's not what you wanted to hear, but I've given it a lot of thought. I've changed my mind and I really don't want children messing up what we have together."

Her heart beat a faster rhythm as he disentangled himself. He jumped up, walked out of the room without saying a word, and slammed the door behind him.

***

She'd seen too many of her friends bogged down with babies, nappies, and drudgery. They'd turned from fun-loving adventurous girls into screeching harridans, worn out with sleepless nights, round-the-clock feeding, and constant worry every time the kid cried, sneezed, or had a fever. One by one they'd stopped going out to concerts, bars or even just for lunch or dinner, worried that trusted babysitters might morph into full-blown paedophiles overnight.

She knew this baby obsession was just nature's con trick. Women's hormones made them desperate to reproduce themselves, but they soon learned the reality; it was just to ensure that the human race did not die out. Once the baby arrived all her friends had wanted to do was put it back where it came from, but it was too late. Marriages died with the stress of a screaming baby, and Kay was adamant that hers would not. She wanted a life, so...*No. Fucking. Way.*

***

"Am I forgiven yet? I do love you, you know that don't you?"

She shuffled over towards him as he climbed into bed, on edge with his constant silence and the need to desperately seek his approval of some kind of childless utopia. She felt a slight flinch as she placed one hand on his chest. He turned his head away from her as he spoke in an unusually flat monotone.

"Kay, I'm having trouble coming to terms with what you've told me. When we first met I had no idea you felt this way about children."

She knew their relationship had just undergone perhaps the biggest blow it would ever take. She slid her hand around his waist and sighed as she put her head on his shoulder.

"I'm sorry, but I didn't know *what* I felt back then. From what I've seen of friends, babies come between couples, not bring them closer together. I want it to be just *us*. We've got a great life now, don't spoil it and turn me into some kind of baby-making machine just so I can fill up all our bedrooms. And, for your information, there's all the things it does to the body. I listened to my mum for long enough – prolapse, piles, varicose veins, figure like a sack of potatoes – no thanks."

She gently cupped his chin and pulled until they were face-to-face. She saw a hunger in his eyes, and heard the question only the persistent and brave dare ever ask:

"But will you think about it?"

She nodded reluctantly, and saw a flash of hope cross his features. He smiled.

"Thank you. I'll ask you once more when the time is right, and until then I'll not mention it anymore."

"It's a deal."

She moved on top of him, eager to regain some kind of equilibrium.

CHAPTER 6 - JOHN

John could almost hear the design team rubbing their hands with glee at the expense of the task in front of them… to work with Kay on refurbishing the glut of empty rooms. He was happy to leave it all to them with one exception – his study. He wasn't sure what the 7ft by 8ft room had been used for in the past, but now it was *his* and his alone. He wanted his handiwork spread all over that study like a rash; plain plastered walls painted in duck-egg blue to show off his certificates and trophies to start with. Then would come the matching vertical blinds he could angle to follow the sun, a dark shaggy carpet averse to showing any dirt, a huge Victorian desk with hopefully a secret drawer or two, and a long Chesterfield taking up one wall where he could imitate Wordsworth in vacant mood.

Simon, his agent, was working on his first million and sending ever-increasing emails. However, John knew he could never settle until his writing area was *just so*. This was why he found himself up a ladder painting the high ceiling instead of starting Series Two of *Love's Tangled Web*.

"Percy reckons yellow crushed velvet curtains in our bedroom would set off the grey carpet *beautifully*."

He laughed as Kay stood in the doorway, hand on hip, in perfect imitation of Percival Ye Myint.

"Is that his real name?" John slapped on a liberal coating of emulsion. "Anyway…I'm leaving it all to you. Just don't send him in here."

"So this is where it's all going to be happening?" Kay walked towards the ladder and ran her hand up one leg of his trousers. "Will Ethan finally give Annie one?"

John shook his leg free and prepared to flick the paintbrush in his wife's direction.

"You'll have to wait and see. Will you stop that? I'll fall off the bloody ladder in a minute."

"I'm out of this man-cave!" Kay retreated backwards, her eyes following the paintbrush. "I'm running off with Percy."

***

He stepped down off the ladder, pleased with the outcome. The plasterer had taken out all the lumps and bumps in the walls, and they were now painted just the shade of pale blue that Percy disapproved of. John folded up a dust sheet covering the Axminster and prized Chesterfield, and lifted up the sash window to open it fully, taking care not to leave his fingerprints in the still-wet paint. Rays of afternoon sun warmed his face and to his great surprise illuminated transparent contours of a young woman wearing a kind of lacy neck to ankle nightshirt lying prone on the Chesterfield when he swung back into the room. John blinked twice to ensure his imagination was not playing tricks. Sure enough the woman, unaware and fading slightly on his prized sofa as he watched incredulously, slumbered gently on.

"Fuck-a-doodle-do!" He whistled softly through his teeth and stuck his head out of the door. "Kay! Come and have a look at this!"

Deciding not to call again on hearing his wife in conversation with Percy on the top floor, he gently pulled the door to and studied the countenance before him in repose. It was a young face, no more than twenty four or twenty five. A dark brown plait of hair contrasted with the pristine white smock and fell over one shoulder. Black lashes fluttered against a pale, somewhat wan and sunless skin. A thin, noble nose and full red lips completed the most bizarre sight that John had ever seen in his life.

Footsteps sounded on the bare boards of the mezzanine corridor, and the door flew open. John turned towards Kay, still with his mouth open in astonishment and with one finger pointing at the Chesterfield. Kay shrugged.

"Did you call?" She followed the direction of his finger. "So? It's a Chesterfield! Fancy a quick one on it then?"

John twisted around in alarm as Kay took a running jump towards the sofa and landed square on top of its three squashy cushions, flipping quickly over to lie seductively with one shapely leg draped up along its back. The woman in white, whoever she was, could no longer be seen.

"Well? What are you waiting for?" Kay laughed and undid another button on her blouse. "I haven't got all day!"

John managed a nearly normal chuckle.

"Steady on, Percy's still prowling about. Do your button up."

"Oh God, I left him in the top bathroom when I heard you call. He has a friend who can get us a good deal on one of those long Victorian gentleman's baths with the claw feet. We'll both be able to get in it!!" Kay leapt up from the sofa. "He's probably more likely to be looking at your chest than mine, anyway."

"Who, the friend?" John, bewildered, checked the Chesterfield for any sign of the woman wearing what he supposed must have been a nightdress. "Or Percy?"

"I'll meet you on the sofa later." She gave him a brief kiss. "Tie a knot in it for now."

As his wife ran back upstairs, John sank down onto his office chair and gazed long and hard at where the woman had lain. He had a thumping headache. He rubbed his eyes, wondering whether he had inhaled too many fumes from the gloss paint. He swivelled around in the chair, folded his arms on the desk in front of him, and momentarily laid down his aching head.

A ten minute power nap eased his symptoms somewhat. Coming to with a start, he remembered the vision he had seen and swung around in the chair.

There she was again…as white as her nightshirt but definitely breathing.

John, heart thumping, crept over to the woman and touched a couple of the cool, soft fingers on her left hand with his own. Her lashes fluttered, her body solidified, and he found himself looking into two eyes of a rather unusual cobalt blue. A voice, rather shaky, whispered a question as their owner looked down at her nightshirt in horror.

"Where am I?"

John bit the side of his mouth to confirm he wasn't still asleep and dreaming.

"You're in my study."

The disbelieving woman was close to tears.

"Your *study*? But this is my bedroom! How did you get here? Did I walk in my sleep? Who *are* you?"

Her form began to fade. John screwed up his eyes and then opened them again in disbelief; she had become translucent. He touched her hand, and her body reassembled as the energy flowed between them. He kept hold of her fingers.

"I'm John Finbow, the owner of this house. What's your name? What year were you born?"

Emily's voice shook as she got to her feet.

"Emily Cuthbertson. I was born January the twenty eighth in the year of our Lord eighteen and forty two."

Warmth from her hand spread into his own as John recalled a quick perusal of the deeds and several generations of Cuthbertsons.

"And I was born September the fifth nineteen fifty seven."

He looked at her features for the expression of surprise, which arrived with some alacrity.

"But that cannot be! Queen Victoria is still on the throne! How can she still be queen in nineteen fifty seven?"

He wanted to wipe away a tear that ran down her cheek.

"It's nearly forty years on from that. "John shook his head. "If I remember rightly, Victoria died almost a hundred years ago."

The woman stared at him open-mouthed, and the door flew open. John instinctively let go of Emily's hand on seeing Kay's eyes darting about the room.

"Who are you speaking to?"

Men in white coats with jackets that fasten at the back were never far from his mind.

"I'm going over a scene I'm writing. It's better if I talk it through."

"Oh." Kay, mollified, shot him a smile. "Do you want me to help?"

"I'm done now." John took a quick glimpse to his right. "Let's go and talk claw baths with Percy."

CHAPTER 7 - EMILY

March winds rattled the sash window, and Emily, lying under the counterpane in a state of sleeplessness, stared at the ceiling. On the ground floor she could hear Peggy scraping out the parlour grate. Before long the birds would start their morning chorus, Lionel's voice would rumble up through the floorboards as he talked pleasantries with Peggy, and then it would be time to attend to her mother's wants and needs for the rest of the day. She thought back to what had happened during the night, and knew she had not been asleep when she met the man who had not yet been born.

She liked the way his greying dark hair was cropped at the back of his head but left longer on the top. She realised that she had seen him before, walking out of the front door into the garden. The clothes were the same; trousers of a kind of blue cotton twill, and a crisp white shirt with knife-edge creases in the sleeves that only a wife would be able to iron in.

Was he married? Emily remembered kindly grey eyes and heat from his hand warming her body. She decided to open up her long-abandoned watercolour set during her mother's afternoon nap time, and try to capture his likeness.

***

She could tell that Beattie was in that interesting condition again as she stepped down from the carriage holding Amelia. She recalled arranging a vase of flowers in one of the guest bedrooms while being shocked by William Dugdale's literature on display, and tried hard not to think of her sister and Alfred locked in the kind of marital bliss she would never experience. She took her little niece from Beattie and gave her a kiss. The toddler giggled as Emily placed her carefully back down on the ground and ruffled her hair.

"It's so lovely to see you all!"

Alfred waved with one hand and held on to the horse's reins with the other.

"I'll take Rubin to the livery stable."

Emily embraced her sister, noticing the first tinges of grey in Beattie's dark curls, which were scraped back into a sensible but practical bun.

"Mama's so looking forward to seeing you!"

Beattie stepped back and looked at Emily questioningly.

"Is she still bedridden?"

"Some of the time." Emily nodded. "Although she does get up quite a lot now."

Beattie smiled.

"Good. Life has to go on, with or without Papa."

And it obviously has for you. Emily wondered if she should make reference to her sister's bulging belly, still visible despite voluminous skirts, but decided against it. She held Amelia's hand and linked her other arm through Beattie's as they strolled towards the front door.

"Lionel moved the beds around, so you and Alfred can have your old room. There's a cot in there too, for Amelia."

"We don't mind where we sleep. It's only for the weekend."

Emily felt a sting of disappointment; by Sunday evening they would be gone again. However, she decided not to think about the emptiness their departure would bring. She stepped lightly into the rectory with Beattie, who embraced a smiling Delia in the hallway.

"Mother!" Beattie feigned surprise. "Lovely to see you up and about!"

Delia appeared pleased at the embrace, and afterwards stooped to embrace her granddaughter, also ignoring Beattie's advanced pregnancy.

"Emily told me you would all be coming today. How's little Amelia?"

"Sleeping better at night now. We're not so tired all the time."

"The Lord is merciful."

"No." Beattie shook her head. "Amelia is."

***

Soon after luncheon she was surprised to find Beattie barging into her room just like she always used to do.

"I've put Amelia down for a nap. Mama is resting, and Alfred is talking to Lionel. What are you painting?"

Emily moved her left arm across the picture, but she was not quick enough. Beattie had seen all.

"Who's he?"

"His name is John Finbow." Emily blushed, and her heart beat a little faster. "Don't say anything to Mama."

Beattie lifted up the likeness and made an approving grunt.

"Nice hair. Is he your beau? He's dressed a little strangely. No hat or beard!"

Emily shook her head, but was eager to converse about her experience.

"He comes to the house sometimes."

"A tradesman?" Beattie looked questioningly at Emily.

"Not exactly…" Emily sighed. "I see him when I'm asleep. But he won't be born for almost another ninety years. His birth year is nineteen fifty seven."

A perplexed frown crossed Beattie's forehead.

"Are you sickening for something?"

"Not at all." Emily smiled at her sister. "He's the man of my dreams."

Amelia gave a cry, causing Beattie to make for the door.

"I'll be back presently to find out more."

She listened to her sister's footsteps ascending to the next floor, and then retrieved her paintbrush. John's grey eyes bored into hers from their two-dimensional state, born into a world she would never be part of. She wiped away a tear and yearned for the caress of night time.

CHAPTER 8 - JOHN

Lying in post-coital bliss with Kay's head on his shoulder and one of her legs draped over his thighs, John gave his wife a contented squeeze and decided to broach the forbidden subject one more time.

"I love you. You'd make a wonderful mother."

He thought he heard the faintest snort of disapproval emanating from the depths of his chest hair.

"I don't think so." Kay lifted herself up on one elbow. "John, you know how I feel about children. I love you too, but I'm not maternal. Please don't keep going on about it."

His disappointment was overwhelming. To have to go through life with no sons or daughters to nurture was more than he could bear. He closed his eyes lest Kay could see a river of tears forming. His voice sounded shaky when he eventually spoke.

"That's the end of that, then."

He felt her head flop back down upon his shoulder.

"So sorry, it's just that I've had a bit more time to think about it, and … I'm happy with the life we have. Please forgive me."

Anger was threatening to put words in his mouth that he would later regret. He sat up, swung his legs over the side of the bed, and reached for his dressing gown.

"I'm just going to make a cup of tea. Want one?"

"No thanks." Kay yawned. "I'm sleepy."

He padded down to the kitchen, switched on the kettle and punched the wall; the stinging pain in his hand deflated his anger somewhat. Blowing on his knuckles, he took a cold beer out of the fridge and flicked the kettle off before returning upstairs. Light snoring came from the direction of the bedroom. He wandered into his study, took a gulp of beer, sat down at his desk and sighed. The reflection on his monitor picked out a familiar supine figure upon the Chesterfield.

John swung the chair around and sprang up. He reached for Emily's hand, and her transparent form solidified before his eyes.

"Hello Emily." He chuckled and kept hold of her fingers. "I'm sure my wife thinks I've started talking to myself."

Her cobalt eyes blinked in recognition, and with a whisper of a smile she sat up.

"My sister likes your hair."

"Eh?" John looked around. "Where is she?"

"I painted your likeness. She looked at that."

John's anger had been replaced with an altogether more pleasurable sensation.

"Can I see it?"

Emily pointed with her free hand.

"Your desk is where my bureau stands. Have a look on that thing behind you."

An accurate replica of his features rested on top of his computer keyboard. John attempted to pick up the picture, laughing as it dissolved through his hands.

"You're a very talented artist."

"I might have the chance to illustrate an epistolary novel, being written by my brother's friend Wilkie Collins."

John's surprise was genuine.

"Really? Is it called *The Moonstone*?"

Emily got to her feet and pointed with her free hand."

"I don't know. He hasn't finished it yet. What *is* that contraption?"

John followed her line of direction.

"It's a computer – like a typewriter but better. I type my novels on it."

"I've read about the new-fangled typewriters." Emily replied. "Mama won't have one in the house. So you're a writer?"

"I write screenplays for TV and film." John nodded but then realised why Emily's expression remained blank. "Sorry, I'm a playwright."

"We both create." Emily smiled. "You with words and myself with pictures, but so far my paintings are just a way to pass the time."

John could not help but ask the question that begged an answer.

"When did you die?"

Her reply shocked him to the core.

"I'm not dead!" Emily's features took on an air of indignation. "It's eighteen and sixty seven and I'm twenty five years' old! I'm too young to die! Look around you – you're in my bedchamber *and* wearing only a dressing gown! If Mama knew you were here she would call the police!"

Her fingers felt warm and solid. John gazed past Emily to the Chesterfield, which had changed to a narrow iron bedstead complete with mattress, pristine bedlinen, and topped with an obvious hand-quilted cover. Embers of an earlier fire burned in the grate. Watercolour paints and a sketchbook were laid out on the fold-down lid of a teak bureau. A jug and bowl stood on a washstand next to the bed. A home-made multi-coloured rag rug covered up polished floorboards in the centre of the room.

John's head spun, causing him to utter the first words that came into his head.

"W.T.F dot com!"

"Pardon?" Emily looked at him blankly. "I don't understand what you're saying. Sit down on the bed – you're looking a little pale."

He let go of her fingers and sank down onto the quilt. When Kay burst through the door the next morning and ran to sit beside him, he rose up with a start and realised he had spent the entire night asleep on the sofa.

"Sorry about last night." Kay hit her forehead with the palm of her hand. "But there isn't any other way of breaking it to you gently. But I *do* love you – very much. Will you come back to bed tonight? *Please* don't be mad at me."

John rubbed his eyes.

"I made a cup of tea and sat down to drink it, but must have dozed off."

"Forgive me?" Kay slipped her arms around his middle. "I *have* thought long and hard about this."

He sighed and leaned his head against hers.

"I know you have. I have to admit it's a great disappointment."

Kay's arms tightened around him.

"But we'll still stay together, yeah?"

"Of course." John nodded. "We're married, aren't we?"

He wondered if he'd made the biggest mistake of his life

CHAPTER 9 - EMILY

She found herself making excuses during the day to sneak into her room, in order to unlock the bureau's secret drawer and gaze at her new friend's likeness. She knew Beattie was desperate to discover the man's identity, but she could tell her no more than she already knew. In her half-world of dreams, she remained unsure as to whether John Finbow even existed at all.

Her sister's inquisitiveness came to a head on the Sunday afternoon as they sat together in the parlour. Emily, unprepared, was embarrassed and affronted beyond belief at Beattie's indelicacy.

"Emily has a beau. Did you know that, Mother?"

Delia's face assumed an expression of horror, as Emily blushed and shook her head.

"It was a dream. Beattie's made a mistake."

Lionel shot Beattie a disapproving look.

"If Emily does have a beau, then I'm sure she'll tell us in her own time."

"Who will look after me if Emily marries?" Delia wailed. "I'll be here all alone!"

Emily stood up and pushed her chair back, ignoring Beattie's crestfallen features."

"Lionel is here, and although the other boys are abroad, I'm sure Beattie,

Eliza and Catherine will all visit as much as they can. Alfred, it was nice to see you and Amelia, but please can you take Beattie home after tea."

In high dudgeon, Emily sailed past her sister and fled upstairs to her room, but an inevitable tentative knock could be heard after a low rumble of voices had died down. Emily locked the secret drawer, laid down on the bed and closed her eyes.

"Come in."

The door opened slowly.

"So sorry." Beattie's voice whispered. "I've just popped in to say goodbye."

Emily kept her eyes shut.

"Goodbye."

"I didn't mean to pry." Beattie whispered. "Forgive me?"

Emily opened her eyes, stared at her sister, and then propped herself up on one elbow.

"Why did you act so thoughtlessly?"

"I don't know." Beattie shrugged. "My brain is all over the place at the moment. I blame it on my condition."

"I want no word of this to go to the rest of the family." Emily flopped back down again. "You are forgiven. Now go."

***

His computer overshadowed the various hues of her watercolour set and there he was, waiting for her again, just like before. Emily smiled.

"Hello John." She sat up on the sofa and looked down. "At least I'm wearing my day clothes this time."

She took his outstretched hand, warming up as he spoke in the soft timbre she had come to admire.

"Because it's only five o'clock."

"Yes." She nodded. "I was horrible to Beattie though. Oh, how I wish Father were still alive."

She enjoyed the sensation of him caressing the back of her hand.

"Who's Beattie?"

"My sister." Emily looked up shyly before continuing. "I was hoping I'd see you again."

"Me too."

Both of her hands were now in his, and she gazed unashamedly at his features, as though memorising each curve for future reference.

"Do you know, you're standing here as solid as *I* am!"

She laughed.

"Why wouldn't I be? I'm not a ghost!"

She saw his face take on a more serious expression.

"Emily, where is your father buried?"

She tried to follow his line of thinking, but could only wonder at the reason behind his question.

"Why, in the village churchyard of course. He was the reverend here for many years. Follow me and I'll show you where it is."

***

Bracken, nettles, spring crocuses and snowdrops fought each other for pride of place on top of the moss-covered grave. Emily, still holding John's hand, led him to the stone.

"Here's Father's resting place. Why do you want to see it? It looks more overgrown than I remember though."

She was surprised to see him searching nearby.

"Not particularly *that* one." He announced enigmatically. "*This* one!"

She took a closer look and felt slightly dizzy.

'Emily Maud Cuthbertson.

Born January 28th 1842

Died April 12th 1868

Rest in the arms of the Lord.

"That's my name! It cannot be!" She shook her head emphatically. "I'm going to die *next year?*"

She felt a rising panic that she could not control, and burst into a flood of tears. Straight away his arms enfolded her.

"Hush. I had to show it to you, so that you realise what's happening. This is the year nineteen ninety six. You've already died, but somehow the energy between us causes you to stay alive in my world. I'm so glad that you do though."

She felt more alive than she had ever been in her own time. The nearness to his body was causing the most unladylike thoughts to rush through her mind. She stood wrapped in his embrace on top of her grave and lifted her face towards his.

"Never let go of me."

His kiss was soft and gentle, sweeping away her panic in an instant.

***

Kay's voice brought him back from a far-away place where a creased percale sheet had been all that had stood between their nakedness and the early summer morning.

"Why are you still crashing on the settee? Come on, John. This has gone on for far too long now."

He felt a keen sense of guilt for the adultery but figured he'd get away with it, just as long as he didn't talk in his sleep.

"Sorry." He jumped up, yawning. "I couldn't relax and came down to watch a film. It wasn't anything to do with you."

Indeed, he had found solace in a body long since dead, a body who had willingly opened up like a flower despite the strict moral codes and etiquette of her time; a body very much alive who yearned for his touch.

"Do you still love me? Is there somebody else?"

Her anguish at the stark question called for only one answer, which to his surprise now seemed impossible to give.

"Don't be silly. Come here." His arms enfolded Kay's petite frame. He rubbed his nose in the top of her hair and enjoyed the familiar scent of apple shampoo. "It won't happen again."

***

He sought her out during the day instead, when he should have been writing and when Kay was out of the house. His screenplay took a back seat to the heights of passion he could achieve with Emily. He would summon his soul mate, the other half of him, and she would arrive, eager and willing.

CHAPTER 10

What if he was correct? Could she really be dead? After much thought Emily admitted to herself that she never felt hungry, and tried without success to remember the last time she had eaten or drank anything. For confirmation of her demise she realised that her monthly curse had disappeared some time ago, and sadly concluded that dead women did not bleed.

However, when autumn leaves crackled and withered, her belly began to swell with his child. The baby kicked and tumbled about, which proved to her undoubtedly that she was a healthy young woman. Distraught at the scandal and possible ostracization by the villagers, and that Lionel might even lose his esteem and livelihood, Emily decided to say nothing of the pregnancy to her mother, not even to Peggy. She wore looser clothing and was grateful for the onset of winter and the chance to don a few more outer layers.

By Christmastime she could not hide her condition anymore when standing naked before the man she adored.

"John, I am with child; *your* child."

The simple look of joy on her lover's face was worth any amount of possible rejection by the good ladies of the church. She welcomed the touch of his hands on her taut abdomen.

"You're having a baby?"

"*Our* baby. So, you see- there's no way I can be dead!"

She could identify with his puzzled expression – she didn't understand it either. Nevertheless, the baby was a gift from the God she thought had abandoned her. She laid her head on his shoulder and sighed.

"I am so happy."

His reply was not what she wanted to hear.

"You will have to see a doctor so that he can examine you and aid with the birth."

"No." She shook her head. "*You* can help me bring our child into the world when my time comes. Nobody must know. Keep me here in your world. I don't want to go back."

She felt his arms encircle her, keeping her and their baby from harm.

"I wish I could, Emily. I really wish I could."

***

"You're gaining weight."

Despite the inner turbulence at her mother's remark, Emily kept her expression noncommittal as her brain scrambled for a reply.

"I've eaten a lot over the Christmas period."

"Exercise restraint." Lionel looked at her over his horn-rimmed glasses. "The gates of heaven are narrow."

She realised the idea of a pregnant spinster had not even entered their minds. However, whilst wearing her nightshirt she caught Peggy's beady eyes scanning her belly several times. Emily knew that as far as their maid was concerned, the game was up. When Peggy brought a jug of hot water one morning in late January, she steeled herself for the inevitable.

"Are you with child, Miss Emily?"

"Nobody must know." Emily nodded. "Not even Mother."

Peggy sighed.

"I've had three children, all grown now. I can help you when your time comes. Just tell me and then go to my cottage when the pains begin – that's day *or* night. A first baby can take many hours to be born."

Emily, relieved, smiled at Peggy.

"You're very kind. Thank you. Please don't tell anybody."

"No, Miss Emily, but if I can see then so can everybody else."

"Only because I'm wearing a thin nightshirt." Emily climbed out of bed. "Mother just thinks I'm fat."

Peggy chuckled

"What will you do about the baby?"

Emily had thought long and hard regarding this conundrum.

"The baby's father will look after it, and I will visit when I can."

"Yes, Miss." Peggy looked unconvinced. "I'll carry on now with my duties."

***

By early April it had become unseasonably warm. Emily awoke at midnight on the twelfth day of the month; not on John's settee as she had hoped, but to a soaking wet bed and griping pains across her abdomen. With no thought of her mother's possible reaction to her disappearance, she threw on her boots and outer clothing over her nightshirt and, in some distress, made her way through the darkened village to Peggy's cottage.

"Peggy!" She rapped loudly on the door with her knuckles. "It's Emily!"

After an agonising wait, flickering candlelight could be seen through the window as Peggy made her way to the door.

"Miss Emily!" Peggy's face was a picture of consternation. "Come in!"

Bent over double with another pain, Emily, frightened at a lack of control over her body, stumbled inside and held onto the back of a chair for support.

"The baby's coming!"

"It'll be ages yet." Peggy replied. "I'll stoke up the fire if you're cold. You make yourself as comfortable as you can. The pains are natural. Go with them and don't fight it."

"I'm not cold! I want John!" Emily cried. "I need him here!"

Peggy, curiosity as far under wraps as she could keep it, ventured a few words.

"Where does he live, Miss? I could go and ask him to come."

"He's at the rectory with me!" Emily screwed up her eyes in pain. "He lives in the twentieth century! He won't come now because I'm not lying in bed!"

Agitated beyond belief, she laid down on the horsehair sofa and felt the back of Peggy's hand against her forehead and heard a gentle whisper in her ear.

"I ought to call the doctor."

Emily shook her head.

"I'm not delirious! Truly I'm not."

"Yes, Miss Emily." Peggy whispered. "Let's get those outer things off and then we can see what's going on."

***

From faraway she could hear a familiar voice as she drifted in and out of consciousness.

"The doctor's here, Miss Emily. I had to call him because only the baby's shoulder is out, and you're losing a lot of blood."

She didn't really care. All she wanted was somebody to stop the grinding pains. She smelled the rubber of a mask as it was placed over her nose and mouth. Doctor Heslop, whom she realised would doubtless go straight to her mother, spoke in an authoritative tone.

"Chloroform, Miss Cuthbertson. I'm going to try and get the baby out."

She floated up to the ceiling with her son and gazed dispassionately at the doctor, who after some manipulations of her body shook his head. Peggy let out a shriek in the certain knowledge that she would have to break the news to Delia. Emily began to run towards John, waiting patiently for her beyond the fog.

PART TWO
AUGUST 1998

CHAPTER 11 - JOHN

Robbie's giggle was always a joy to his ears. John rolled the ball with its Manchester United logo towards the little boy, fruit of his loins, whom Kay would never know. The smile on his child's face mirrored his own contentment at the realisation that if somebody wanted something badly enough, then sooner or later they would find a way to obtain it.

"Roll it back to Daddy."

He could see that his son was turning out to be the very image of him. In his scrutiny of the infant's features he missed the sound of his wife approaching from behind.

"Who are you talking to?"

He jumped up and turned around to face Kay. He had summoned his little playmate, and Robbie had appeared. The energy between the three of them was so intense that his touch was no longer needed to keep them in sight. However, now he had to block the sight of the ball gaining momentum all by itself. The ball hit his ankle and he kicked it away. Out of the corner of his eye he saw Robbie, followed faithfully by Emily, run on sturdy toddler legs to pick it up before making his way back towards him.

"Oh, nobody." John shrugged. "I was just thinking aloud."

Kay placed two mugs of tea on a small table in between their garden loungers and plonked herself down. She stretched out on the long chair and closed her eyes like a cat in the sun.

"I'm getting worried about you. I keep on hearing you talking to yourself. This isn't the first time it's happened, John."

He was glad her eyes were shut and that she could not see the expression on his face. He took the ball from Robbie's pudgy hand and let it fall, blew Emily a quick kiss, and made his way over to the lounger. Emily, realising his tricky situation, held Robbie's hand and stood back.

"I'm okay, really I am." He sat down and took a sip of tea. "I like going over lines aloud instead of in my head."

"No." Kay turned to face him and opened her eyes. "I heard you say *roll it back to Daddy!*"

His heart skipped a beat. He could have sworn she was still at work. He must have been engrossed in playing ball. He had no idea how to reply, and so remained silent.

"I know that you yearn for a child, John. I think the stress of it is starting to affect you mentally. I think you should make an appointment to see the doctor. I know you think all doctors are pervs, but our GP is a very nice lady I can assure you."

In his peripheral vision he saw Robbie pulling Emily over towards a red tricycle. Emily lifted him onto the seat and held onto the back, before pushing a giggling Robbie along their newly tarmacked path.

"You've got it all wrong." He finally mumbled. "I'm used to our life now without children."

"No you're not." Kay sat up and shook her head. "I think we need to discuss our future. I don't want you to live a life full of regrets."

The implication of her words brought him up short.

"Future? What do you mean?"

She fixed him with the stare he'd seen her reserve for those incredibly stupid people unfortunate enough to cross her path.

"Come on, I wasn't born yesterday. There's somebody else, isn't there? You're not writing *anything*. You walk around in a dream most of the time, and you talk to someone for hours on the phone in your study day or night behind a locked door. What am I *supposed* to think? Okay, I know you think I've deceived you about not wanting a child, but I only realised this recently, not when we first got together. Do you love her, this other woman?"

His wife was smarter than he'd given her credit for. Emily came over with Robbie in her arms, and sat down on the grass beside them.

"Tell her about *us*, John." Emily implored and looked up at him. "It's not fair to her."

John sat forward on the lounger with his elbows on his knees, and rested his head in his hands.

"You'll never believe me if I *did* tell you."

"So tell me!" Kay let out a sigh. "Let *me* decide that!"

John nodded and met Kay's gaze with what he hoped was a look of honesty.

"I have a son. He's not alive but he *is* alive, if that makes any sense."

His words struck home like a cricket ball hitting the stumps.

"Why have you never told me this in all the time we've been together?"

Kay's features registered incomprehension. John took a great slurp of tea, relishing the liquid in his throat, which suddenly felt bone dry.

"Because then I didn't have one. Look, I'll show you something."

He stood up and walked over to the ball.

"I'm going to pick this up and roll it to my son. He's nearly two years old. If you keep watching, he'll roll it back."

With the ball in his hand, John walked around to face Robbie, who followed his actions with an inquisitive stare.

"Robbie." John squatted down on his haunches and smiled at the infant. "Stand up and roll the ball back to me."

He let the ball go from his hand. Robbie broke free of his mother's grip, and stood watching until the ball came to a stop.

"Come on Robbie, throw it to Daddy."

He heard Kay gasp as the ball took on a life of its own, thrown with a typical toddler's inaccuracy, and which landed with a thud on top of the sun lounger.

"John…" Kay jumped up in alarm. "What's going on?"

John sat down next to Emily, and let Robbie climb onto his lap.

"I told you. Robbie threw it. *Now* do you believe me?"

Kay looked all around her, a worried expression on her face.

"I don't know what to believe, and don't tell me I had a miscarriage! *Who is his mother, and do I know her?*"

John got to his feet and took Kay's hand.

"Come with me, and I'll show you."

***

He knew she felt uneasy walking along the path towards the back of the churchyard. He wasn't sure whether a sudden breeze or the sight of the ball moving by itself had given her the chills. John held on to Emily's fingers with one hand, and grabbed Kay's hand with his other one. His wife shivered. Robbie ran alongside them, unconcerned.

"What are we here for?"

They stopped by an overgrown grave covered in moss, and he disentangled his fingers from Kay's. He pointed to a tombstone etched faintly with the name *Emily Maud Cuthbertson*, mumbled a few words, and then turned towards his wife.

"Here's Robbie's mother. She lived in our house in the eighteen sixties, but she's standing beside me now, as solid to me as you are. I can see her just as long as I keep hold of her hand."

Kay looked past him in horror, but saw only old unkempt graves covered in lichen and tumbleweed that were set out in a rather random fashion.

"I can't see her, John."

He took her hand again.

"Neither could I until she appeared in my study, which used to be her bedroom. She came to *me*, Kay. I didn't seek her out."

She shook her head in disbelief.

"Okay, so what you're saying is that you've had sex with a ghost? Jesus Christ! Get her to do something then… if I can see the proof with my own eyes then it'll be obvious you're an adulterer and not a raving lunatic!"

The white-hot anger etched into her features faded as a pound coin floated out from his pocket and hovered in front of her eyes. She stretched out trembling fingers to catch it in the palm of her hand, and then watched as if in a dream while it slowly returned to its owner. She shrugged.

"So this is where we sell the house and go our separate ways, I suppose?"

He turned to face her and took both of her hands in his.

"No…it doesn't have to be that way. Emily's life in the house runs parallel to ours, even though we're over a hundred years apart. You've as much right to live there as she has. She's taken me back to Victorian times and I've seen how it was…how it still *is*. It's fascinating, Kay."

"No wife wants to play gooseberry, especially to a fucking ghost!" Kay shook her head. "You're out of your mind! All I see is my husband screwing another woman!"

She broke free of his grip and began to run back along the path, unwilling to let him see the tears already forming behind her eyes. Emily, looking down at her grave, picked up Robbie and clutched him to her breast; her little stillborn boy sweetening the bitter pill of death.

CHAPTER 12 - KAY

"Thank you for seeing me so quickly, Mrs Sedgwick."

Kay followed the medium along a narrow passageway towards an office at the back of a rather upmarket detached house.

"No problem. Call me *Coral*." Coral Sedgwick looked back over her shoulder and smiled. "I had a last minute cancellation."

Kay took in the accreditation certificates and thank-you cards stuck to the walls as she entered the office.

"Sit yourself down, and we can have a chat." Coral pointed towards a full glass standing on a table between them. "There's water for you if you wish."

Kay's nervousness knew no bounds, and she sat on her cold hands briefly to ease their shaking.

"Have you visited a medium before, Mrs Finbow?"

Kay shook her head and smiled at the middle-aged, slightly overweight woman opposite.

"I've never had any reason to. I found your website... well, I saw your name in the newspaper after you'd helped the police find that poor girl, and wondered if you could help *me*."

"I am clairvoyant...I see Spirit, and also clairsentient...I sense them too, so yes, I'll certainly try." Coral nodded. "What seems to be the trouble?"

Exhaling slowly, Kay managed a thin smile.

"This is going to sound utterly ridiculous, but my husband is having an affair with the ghost of a woman, Emily, who used to live in our house."

To her surprise, Coral did not burst into fits of laughter.

"This ghost…have you seen her?"

Kay shrugged.

"Not as such, but I've seen her move a coin. It just floated on air. My husband sits in his study all day and talks to her. We're not really speaking now. It's awful, what's happened to us. The most bizarre thing of all is that he says she's had his baby. Can you do anything? Is *he* mad or am I?"

She hated the sound of her voice, pleading and sounding slightly out of control. The reply when it came poured balm onto her troubled soul.

"Neither probably. Obviously what's needed is for me to pay a visit to your home and encourage Emily to move on from the limbo she seems to have found herself in. Sometimes spirits cannot accept their former bodies are no longer living, and they hang around on the earth plane and make a nuisance of themselves."

"Will she listen to you?" Kay remained unconvinced. "She seems pretty firmly entrenched."

"I usually have a good success rate." Coral nodded. "Er… my rates are forty pounds an hour by the way."

Kay opened her bag and took out a purse.

"That's fine. I can pay you now…let's say two hours to start with. I'll leave you my details, so just phone me when you're able to pay us a visit."

"It shouldn't be too long." Coral took the proffered notes. "Probably the day after tomorrow."

***

She decided to say nothing to John if Coral turned up while she was out of the house, other than she was expecting a visit from an old family friend. As far as she was concerned, John hardly seemed to notice she was there anyway. Kay had given up on trying to paper over the cracks of any damage caused by her outburst, and waited impatiently for Coral to remove Emily's spirit and restore some peace and tranquillity to their lives.

And so it was with some trepidation that she opened the door to Coral two days' later.

"Come in. John's in the study as usual, talking to *her*. I can hear him through the wall."

Coral breezed into the hallway.

"We'll get to work straight away, Mrs Finbow. I can already sense a spirit presence here, by the way."

Kay took the stairs to the mezzanine floor two at a time, ignoring the medium's heavy breathing behind her. She tapped lightly on the study door, aware of a sudden silence on the other side.

"What?"

She turned the handle and popped her head around the door, noticing a selection of children's toys scattered about on the carpet.

"I want to introduce you to somebody."

John sat up quickly from his prone position on the sofa.

"Who?"

There was suspicion in his eyes, causing Kay to wonder whether Coral was their last chance at reparation.

"This is Coral. She's a medium. There's no other way of saying this…she's come to send Emily and Robbie back to where they ought to be so that we can get on with our lives. You haven't been yourself for a long time, John. Emily's come between us."

She was unprepared for the response. The door flew open, pulled from her hand by an unseen energy, a force causing Coral to topple backwards while John leapt towards her in anguish.

"No! Emily is the mother of my son! She won't be going anywhere!" He pointed a finger a Coral, who climbed shakily to her feet. "Get her out of my house!"

A red toy train began to chug slowly across the carpet towards the door, pushed by something Kay could not see. Her eyes locked in horror with John's. Coral's strident voice boomed across the mezzanine landing.

"Emily! It's time to leave the Earth plane and move on! Go in peace in the name of the Lord!"

With a superhuman effort Kay tore herself away from her husband's gaze, hardly aware of the trickle of urine down the inside of her legs at the sudden sight of a pale, twenty five year old woman with long dark hair. The woman held onto a small infant, who clutched a red toy train. Both of them appeared in the exact spot on the landing where Coral had just been standing.

John looked down at the wet patch on the carpet, and then at his wife's frozen features.

"You don't need to be alarmed, Kay. Emily has been waiting many years for this. It's okay, *really* it is."

He smiled at the two most important women in his life, and took the solid, warm body of Robbie from Emily and into his arms.

"Daddy's here, Robbie." He kissed his son's head. "We're going to have so much fun you and I. We'll be just one big happy family."

With the little boy's arms around his neck, John felt happier than he had been in a long time despite the expression on Kay's face.

"You sick *fuck*!" Kay screamed at Emily. "What have you done with Coral?"

"I am she." Emily's voice took on Coral's tonation, as she stepped forward to stand beside John. "Coral was a vexation. Robbie and I sapped her spirit energy. How could she even *think* of separating a child from its father?"

John wracked his brain for a way of reconciling the two women. All he had ever wanted stood in front of him now; he had all the money he needed, and a house big enough for the four of them. *Why were women never content?*

"I'm going to Google exorcisms." Kay's voice wavered as she stared at Emily. "And then we'll see how long it takes for Coral to return. If you think you're sleeping in my bedroom, you can think again. You will *never* kick me out of my own house!"

"*Google?*" Emily turned worriedly to John. "What does she mean?"

"I'll explain later." John ran a hand distractedly through his hair. "Kay, nobody is going to make you leave, unless you actually want to."

"Yes I bloody well want to!" Kay turned to him with venom. "But no way am I going to leave Coral alone here until that..." She pointed a finger at Emily. "....that *thing* has gone from her body. It was my idea to bring a medium here, it's my fault what's happened to her, and I'm going to do my best to get Coral back."

"You *know* I will actively discourage you in any way I can." John hoped his voice sounded threatening enough. "Emily is the mother of my son."

Kay, aware of her clothes now uncomfortably wet, pulled herself up to her full height and relished the half inch advantage that allowed her to look slightly down on Emily.

"Who knows how many men she's been shagging on the other side? That kid could be anyone's."

"Well, he isn't." John shook his head. "He's mine, and you will just have to get used to it."

"She might look sweet and innocent." Kay shot another venomous stare at Emily. "But she's taken you over completely. All she's been looking for is a body to jump into. She's evil, John."

As far as he was concerned, no person more loving than Emily could have walked the earth. John gave a shuddering sigh, willing his ordeal over.

"Kay, we seem to have come to the end of the road. I don't care about this house, you can have it. Emily and I will take Robbie and we'll go somewhere else. I don't want to hurt you any more than I have already."

"This is *my* house!" Emily interjected. "No way am I moving anywhere! I've been here nearly a hundred years before you two were even born!"

Impasse deepened a strained silence, broken only by Robbie's toy train crashing to the floor. Kay, unnerved beyond belief, turned on her heel and ran into the bedroom, slamming the door behind her.

***

Wrapped in a towel, she stepped out from the en-suite shower to find John, dejected, sitting bolt upright on the bed.

"I'm so sorry. We'll take one of the other bedrooms upstairs. Emily's adamant that she's staying here."

Kay shrugged and fastened the towel more securely.

"I'm not moving either, not until Coral's back."

"Then you'll have a long wait." John stood up and made for the door. "I'm sorry it's come to this."

Kay stuck a middle finger up at her husband's retreating back.

CHAPTER 13 - JOHN

Little Robbie fulfilled a need in him that was somehow primitive. John purchased a state-of-the-art digital camera and camcorder, and snapped away as the boy played, proud to be just like any other doting father.

"Look, Emily." He held the camera towards her and clicked through the photos. "Our boy's first pictures. I've taken moving pictures too, which are called videos. Here... have a look."

Unwilling to take the camcorder from him, Emily watched her son kick a ball and then run towards the camera.

"How is this so?"

"Ha, ha." John waggled a finger at her. "Twenty first century technology."

She reluctantly turned away from the cameras and smiled at him.

"Father had daguerreotypes made when we were children. This is...almost magical."

"Come with me." John gestured with his free hand. "I'll show you some more magic."

He relished their time together whilst Kay was at work and Robbie had his afternoon nap. The Chesterfield exuded the comforting smell of old leather as he opened the study door. With Emily standing at his side he sat down and switched on the computer.

"I'll upload the photos and video, save them to a folder, and you'll see them on the screen here." He tapped the monitor and laughed. "Photography's advanced a little bit since your time."

"Not only photography." Emily replied with a sigh. "Nothing is familiar. I'm lost, unable to cook even a simple meal. I feel useless and overwhelmed. The cars in the road outside frighten me. Everything is difficult."

"You'll learn." John clicked onto a new folder. "I'll print out these photos in a minute and you can keep them."

He stared, quite unbelieving, at the monitor. The first picture taken in the back garden showed an empty path constructed of crazy-paving. He unplugged the USB cable and checked the camera's corresponding photo. Robbie sat on his tricycle; one foot on the grass and the other on the crazy-paving.

"What the fuck?"

He clicked onto the next photo in the folder. To his horror, Coral stood on the grass where Emily should have been.

"I'm not there!" Emily wailed. "Neither Robbie nor I are in the pictures!"

"But you're here on the camera!" John shook his head, perplexed, and pressed the forward arrow on the camera "Look! You can see for yourself!"

"I do not exist!" Emily began to cry as she looked at her image and then up at the monitor. "It's true! I'm dead!"

He stood up and wrapped his arms around her.

"Not any more you're not. You're a living, breathing woman and I love you."

Her response to his kiss blew away any doubts. He picked her up in his arms, and carried her upstairs.

CHAPTER 14 - KAY

Kay unlocked the front door quietly. She was tired and felt as though she was incubating one of her sore throats. Tim had allowed her to go home early, and she needed to soak in a hot bath. She listened, but there was no sound in the house. She kicked off her shoes and went up to her bedroom on the mezzanine floor.

Unusually, the door to the study was open. Kay, intrigued, suppressed a sneeze and popped her head inside. The computer screen was frozen, depicting an image of Coral standing in what she recognised was their back garden, wearing the same clothes that Kay had last seen her in.

A sound echoed from the upstairs landing. Robbie had awoken from his nap, and Kay knew there was no time to lose. She wiggled the mouse to free the picture, and searched around until she found a memory stick. Hearing Emily's voice above, she hurriedly copied the folder of photos and then ran to her bedroom and closed the door.

Lying back in the bath, she mused on whether the date embedded in the folder's properties could be used as proof that Coral was alive, or conversely whether the police might arrest her and John if they ever saw the photo of Coral standing there as large as life in their garden some days after somebody had decided to report her missing.

She saw the newspaper article a week later as she ate her lunch at work in Tim's small office kitchen, about how the family of missing Coral Sedgwick were offering a reward for any information which might lead to the medium's discovery. Kay chewed thoughtfully on her sandwich and wondered if the police, who were now involved, would believe the story she had to tell. She wrote down the family's contact email address given at the end of the article, and tried to concoct a plausible explanation in her head.

However, fate was to intervene after the front doorbell's chimes brought Emily out into the entrance hall later that week. Kay peeped over the landing balcony and recognised Dave Secombe, Village Constable, below.

"Good evening. Can I speak to Mrs Kay Finbow please?"

She waited until Emily was halfway up the stairs before she descended, noticing irritation splashed across the younger woman's features. As she came face to face with Constable Secombe, Kay was aware of Emily's presence immediately behind her.

"Hi Dave." Kay quickly stepped out into the garden and closed the front door. "What can I do for you?"

If the constable thought her action strange, he showed no sign of it.

"Kay, I need to speak to you regarding the disappearance of Coral Sedgwick. You've read about it in the papers I'm sure."

"Yes I have." Kay nodded. "I've been trying to think of a way to tell you what I know."

"Your name and address was the last one in her diary." Dave Secombe opened a notebook. "Did she arrive here?"

The front door flew open wide to reveal John striding towards her.

"Hi Dave." John grasped the constable's hand and shook it warmly. "What's up?"

"I was asking your wife if she'd seen Coral Sedgwick, the missing medium. Did she arrive at your house last week?"

"Not to my knowledge." John shook his head. "What about you, Kay?"

His eyes glittered. Kay's heart sank.

"No." Her eyes met Dave Secombe's imploringly. "I haven't seen her."

"What about the other lady I just spoke to?" The constable looked towards the front door. "Could she add anything?"

"She's a family friend staying here for a while." John waved to Emily standing in the doorway. "She only arrived a few days ago."

That bit was true anyway. Kay resolved to send an email to Coral's family as soon as she could.

***

"So you see, Emily sapped Coral's spirit energy, which must have been momentarily weak at the time because she was caught off guard I think. I know this all sounds like absolute lunacy, but Coral is in my house, trapped inside Emily who has taken over her body."

Peter Sedgwick's mouth formed an 'o' of surprise. Kay hoped Coral's husband did not immediately send for men to arrive holding white jackets with sleeves that fastened at the back.

"I know about this!" Peter exclaimed excitedly, and pushed back strands of grey hair from his forehead. "Coral's talked about it before. Are you absolutely sure this is what's happened?"

"I saw it with my own eyes. "Kay nodded. "*And* I wasn't dreaming. I've got photos with me on a memory stick that John took only a few days' ago, probably of Emily, but Coral is standing there instead. Emily had been waiting in our house since the eighteen sixties for the right person, and she found her soul mate in my husband who was desperate for children. So was she, but unfortunately I don't want kids. I wish to God I could change my mind now, but I still feel the same way."

"Coral's a strong spirit." Peter patted Kay's arm. "She'll overcome Emily sooner or later. It's all a question of her finding the strength and the right moment. If I can visit your house I'll try to tune into Coral's energy. I'm clair audient only, so I can only *hear* Spirit. We met at a spiritualist convention thirty years' ago, you know. I'll have a look at those photos if you don't mind."

She had been believed!

"Not at all. Peter…can we do anything else to help?" She gazed around Coral's front room and felt a small frisson of elation. "Contact a priest?"

Peter shrugged.

"You could do, but it might only make matters worse. If I can be in the same room as Emily I'll be able to contact Coral I'm sure, and help her positive energy to rise above Emily's. You said there's a child too?"

Kay nodded.

"Yes. A toddler, Robbie. We'll have to do this when John's not about though. He's too involved and he will try and stop you. The trouble is, he hardly ever leaves Robbie's side."

"Nobody will be able to stop me contacting Coral, but I need to be in close proximity to Emily for it to work. You won't hear me speak, but I'll be able to talk to Coral via vibrational energy." Peter sat back in his armchair. "Don't worry. There's no point contacting the police either. They'll cart you away."

Kay gave a wry laugh.

"Yes, that's what put me off talking to Dave Sedgwick. You must admit, to the average bod this whole thing sounds preposterous."

"All I can say is thanks for that email." Peter gave Kay a smile. "I was beginning to get a little worried."

CHAPTER 15 - KAY

She now always felt in the way in her own house. Kay was happier out in the garden, especially when she knew John was attempting to write again and the little boy was careering around the passageways on his tricycle followed by Emily. Two women in one home did not bode well for family harmony.

Kay, watched by Peter, raked up fallen leaves until she saw Robbie appear on the patio. She usually skirted around the boy, but on this occasion picked up a child's rake from the grass, staring past him until she could see Emily framed in the back doorway.

"Come and help me rake up the leaves, Robbie!"

She knew her voice sounded maniacally false and shrill, but to her relief the toddler took the bait. Peter stood up from his seat on a garden bench and Kay's heart began to race. Emily, wearing a long Victorian skirt and a high-necked blouse, followed behind Robbie and then stared at Peter with interest.

"Is this your friend?"

"Yes." Kay nodded. "His name is Peter."

"Hi." Peter met Emily's gaze. "Nice to meet you."

"Is Robbie bothering you?" Emily walked in front of them towards the toddler. "I can take him away if you prefer."

Kay moved to the side as Peter fixed his eyes on Emily's back.

"No, he's fine just where he is. Robbie, you can put the leaves in the wheelbarrow over there."

The boy flashed a smile and then slowly vanished. The child's rake dropped to the ground and Emily began to sway.

"No! I will *not!*"

Peter took a deep breath, closed his eyes, and Emily crumpled to the ground.

"Go in peace, Emily." Peter loomed over the fallen body. "Move towards the light."

Emily's limbs thrashed in protest, and withered autumn leaves created a whirlwind effect around her. Kay stepped back from the force of something unseen, as the young woman's outer form metamorphosed into the stocky figure of Coral. The medium opened her eyes, blinked, and then rose like an injured phoenix from amongst the fallen leaves, straight into the arms of her husband.

"We must go quickly." Coral's voice trembled. "Emily's energy is too strong for me. She's still standing here, shouting and blaspheming. Who'd have thought a vicar's daughter could curse so well? Robbie's spirit is weak, and he's gone. It's my belief and hope that Emily will soon follow him.

"Together we've won." Peter kissed Coral's forehead. "We have you back where you belong."

***

There was no time to lose; Kay could hear John's voice through the open study window calling for Robbie. She sat as sedately as she could manage at the kitchen's breakfast bar, whilst Peter and Coral's feet beat a tattoo on the gravel path down the side of the house. She exhaled a pent-up breath as the roar of their BMW's engine sprang to life.

"Where's Emily and Robbie?"

John, flustered, appeared in the kitchen and looked at her accusingly. Kay swallowed a phantom lump in her throat.

"Gone a-haunting in the garden last I saw of them." She replied airily. "Robbie's raking up leaves, I think."

He pushed past her.

"Ha ha. Very funny."

She decided to sit it out and wait for the inevitable. Within a few moments the back door flew open with a force not unlike that of a hurricane.

"They're not there!"

Kay idly turned the page of a magazine.

"Perhaps she's gone back to her grave."

John came in closer to Kay and loomed over her menacingly.

"If you know where they are, I'd appreciate it if you could tell me."

"How the fuck would I know?" Kay got to her feet and stepped backwards. "I try and keep out of her way most of the time."

As dignified as she could be under the circumstances, Kay picked up her magazine and sauntered nonchalantly out of the kitchen.

***

She could hear him crying through the walls of the study. Slowly she opened the door to see him distraught, lying down on the Chesterfield with one hand held up at an odd angle.

"Where are you, Em?"

"She's gone."

He sat up with a start. In the depths of his misery she knew he had not heard her enter the room. She walked cautiously over to the settee and he moved his feet to one side. She sat down and sighed.

"I lied earlier on. I *do* know where Emily is."

"You do?" His eyes met hers with hope. "Tell me!"

Kay ran a hand distractedly through her hair.

"She was a ghost, John, who has now moved on to find Robbie and hopefully end up where she's supposed to be. Coral's husband came here and his energy was strong enough to bring Coral back. I can't carry on living here now, knowing I'm not the most important person in your life anymore. I know you can't stand the sight of me, and so I've decided to rent a flat."

She willed him to say anything that might her give a clue as to how he felt. However, he lay silently back down, closed his eyes, and turned his face to the wall.

CHAPTER 16 - KAY

She had never lived on her own. Kay turned a key in the lock of her rented flat and stood on the step, unwilling to close the door and shut herself off once again from the rest of the world. She had grown up with the noise of four siblings and a large extended family in close proximity on the Broadberry estate, and now her new flat seemed deathly quiet.

However, residing in the old rectory had shown her there was a better standard of living, where police cars were not permanently parked outside on Friday and Saturday nights, and where fire engines were not called on a regular basis to extinguish teenage arsonists' blazes in the tower blocks' rubbish skips. Kay shivered with the realisation that she might be called a *nouveau riche* snob, but never in her wildest nightmares would she ever consider moving back to live near her sisters.

The door clicked shut behind her. She took off her outer coat and walked along a short passageway, mentally counting off the ten strides needed to arrive at a kitchen so compact where she considered that even swinging the proverbial cat might cause its head to hit the walls. Kay switched on the kettle, looked out of the window at the street below, and wondered how to fill the empty hours before bedtime.

She considered catching up with family gossip by calling her sisters, but knew from previous experience that to phone them in the early evening would only interrupt them from feeding and bathing their myriad brood of children. She imagined the noise and bustle inside their homes, and wondered how on earth they managed to carry on as single mothers on benefits. Becoming rich had estranged her from the people she had grown up with, siblings included, who still inhabited the kind of world she had been desperate to escape from. There was also the double whammy of not having lived in Southcombe for long enough to have made any firm friends.

Why was she so against becoming a parent? Kay recalled her own mother complaining in later years how she'd never had any time for herself, functioned on only four hours' sleep every night, and had her youthful body worn out by difficult childbirths and multiple pregnancies. *Had these grievances planted themselves in her brain as fears?* Kay sighed and tried to imagine the pain of giving birth and the terror of delivering a small being that was totally and utterly dependent.

A tasteless supper had been eaten and washed up by seven thirty. She thought of John rattling around the rectory searching for Emily, and wondered about his mental state now that two months had passed with no communication. There was nothing on TV and she still had her key. Christmas was approaching, and she decided the time was right to pay her husband a visit.

***

Armed with a wrapped, framed photograph of the two of them in happier times, Kay walked smartly down the communal stairway towards her car. Brackenrye lay just a few miles from Southcombe, and the wintry black ice so prevalent in January had not yet spread its tendrils on the roads. Her car, parked under a streetlight (a habit left over from her Broadberry days), started first time, and Kay eased away from the kerb with a slight feeling of apprehension at the upcoming meeting.

How had it all come to this? She moved up through the gears and thought back to spending fruitless hours at the Broadberry museum, just hoping to catch sight of him as he went about his business. When she had first seen his lithe figure running up the steps to the museum, she had decided there and then to check him out further. The counter staff had eventually given her a season ticket, but by then they had passed the coffee stage and were on dinners-for-two in romantic restaurants. He'd been cautious, shy and nervous.

She smiled wryly to herself in the darkness of the car; she had been patient and in love. Kay drove along Church Lane until she came to the open iron gates of the rectory, her tyres crunching on the gravel in a familiar way. Light from the entrance porch flooded the front of the garden, but the rest of the house appeared to be unlit. She sounded the old Victorian knocker, and silently let herself in with her key when nobody came to the door, feeling for the hall light to her left as she stepped onto the coir mat. It was not there.

"John?"

Her voice reverberated back from the high ceiling. Kay used the light from her phone to take a quick peek around, noticing empty beer bottles piled up in one corner, an overflowing grate with ash from many log fires, and an overall air of neglect.

Worried, she let herself out and on an impulse fished out a torch from the glove compartment of her car. The road outside was in darkness as the torchlight picked out a path towards the medieval church at the end of the lane. Kay shivered and tried not to feel spooked at the sight of spotlights in the churchyard casting eerie shadows of tombstones in the early evening mist.

Utilising the glare of several arc spotlights, she stepped carefully along the side path to the back of the church, to where a huddled figure came into view lying prone on what she now knew to be Emily Cuthbertson's grave.

"John?"

There was no immediate response. Kay, heart beating faster, hurried to the grave.

"John, it's Kay!" She touched her husband's face. "John, are you alright? Come on home, you're frozen!"

The bundle of clothing moved slightly.

"Go away."

"I can't leave you like this." She shone the torch into his face. "You need help. She's gone. You can't carry on like this."

He flinched away from the light and sat up.

"I come to her grave every evening." He rubbed his eyes. "I feel close to her and Robbie here. Just leave me, Kay. Find somebody else. I'm no good to you now."

She squatted down beside him.

"John, we've been together a long time. I'm really worried about you."

"I'm fine." He stood up. "I had a family which was taken away from me. I'm sure you'd feel bloody depressed as well if it ever happened to you. But hey, there's no worries there, eh?"

He turned away and strode off purposely down the path towards the lane.

***

He found comfort lying on the grave. She was there beneath him and her name was on the tombstone, proof that she had once existed. He took to carrying a sleeping bag under his arm on dry, clement evenings, and always awoke refreshed to the dawn chorus invading his dreams.

A slight irritation quickly escalated at Kay's sudden nightly excursions to the churchyard. At first he pretended to be asleep, but then the shaking began.

"John! This has to stop!"

He unzipped the bag and sat up, exhaling with force.

"What do you want? Why don't you piss off and leave me alone?"

"Can't you see this is morbid? You're not in your right mind, surely? Who the fuck would want to spend a night in December lying on someone's grave?"

"It's not just anyone's grave." John stood up, ignoring stiff muscles. "It's Emily's, the mother of my son."

He strode along the path to the front of the church, but she kept pace.

"Will you come with me and see the GP?"

"Will I *hell.*" He turned into Church Lane. "*You're* the one who needs a check-up from the neck up."

"So where *is* your son then? He hasn't even got a grave!"

She stood by her open car door and he wanted to punch her lights out. His hands balled into fists.

"He's with his mother."

"Exactly." She nodded. "And she's been six foot under for over a hundred years. Look at the dates on her bloody tombstone. Be realistic John! And what's happening at the house? The light switch is missing in the hallway and you haven't cleared out the grate."

"Peggy comes in once a week to clean. She's due tomorrow."

"Peggy? Who the hell's Peggy?"

The church bell chimed eleven o'clock. The noise of it, coupled with Kay's holier-than-thou voice, assaulted his ears.

"My cleaner, so mind your own fucking business."

He stepped towards her menacingly. She jumped into the car, locked the door, and started up the engine.

CHAPTER 17 - KAY

Was she a selfish bitch denying him a child? What was she really afraid of?

She Googled 'childbirth' and started to watch any TV programme on giving birth that she could find. The animalistic grunting and panting made her feel nauseated. Procreating was akin to torture as far as she could tell. It had killed Emily Cuthbertson and had worn her own mother down to a shadow of her former self. Post-pregnancy she would have to endure bovine-like milk encrusted breasts for the sake of a voracious parasite who would suck the life out of them and reduce their shape to that of two wet envelope flaps. Kay could see nothing positive about the whole experience.

Did she require therapy? Kay came to the conclusion that she would need to get back in touch with her siblings and get the lowdown on pregnancy and childbirth. Reluctantly she picked up the phone and invited herself to the house of the most fertile of her sisters, Lana, who so far had provided her with three nieces and two nephews that she had hardly ever seen.

***

What did kids like? Kay didn't have a clue. Armed with an array of jigsaw puzzles, sweets and chocolates, she pulled the car up outside her sister's council house. Abandoned bikes and scooters were scattered in the front garden, along with two overflowing rubbish bins. She stepped over a pair of roller skates and made her way towards a cacophony of noise emanating from behind a front door left slightly ajar.

"Hi!" Kay pushed the door open. "Lana?"

"Hey!" Lana shouted and came towards her, arms outstretched. "Frankie, I told you to shut the front door…anybody could walk in!"

A boy aged about nine or ten with blond hair cut close to his head ran down the stairs.

"Sorry Mum. Who's she?"

"*She*." Lana smiled her sister. "Is your auntie Kay."

Kay looked at the boy in surprise.

"Wow! Is that Frankie? Last time I saw him he was about four!"

"They tend to grow if you feed them." Lana chuckled. "Wait until Barry comes in… he's thirteen now and taller than I am."

Kay fished in her bag and proffered a jigsaw in Frankie's direction.

"I guess he's too old for a puzzle?"

"The girls love puzzles. With the boys it's all about killing people on video games."

"Oh…lovely." Kay pulled a face. "Perhaps you'd like these sweets then?"

Frankie took the sweets from her hand.

"Cool. Thanks. I didn't know I had an auntie Kay."

"Well, you do." Kay smiled at the boy who was the image of her sister. "I'm very pleased to meet you."

The boy gave her an odd look and ran back upstairs.

"Come on in. Excuse the mess." Lana shrugged. "It's a madhouse. They'll all be in for their tea in about an hour. We've got time for a cuppa first."

The kitchen was homely and lived in, and as far as Kay could see had not changed from the last time she had visited. Photos of the children adorned the walls next to the younger ones' paintings. Unwashed plates and cups were piled up on the draining board. Lana placed them in a bowl of hot soapy water.

"I was just starting the washing up, but now you're here we'll have a natter instead. How's it going with you?"

Kay suddenly wanted to cry for no reason that she could fathom. Her voice when she replied sounded unusually croaky.

"Not too good. John and I have separated."

"Bloody men." Lana switched on the kettle. "Who needs the bastards? Not one of my kids' fathers stayed around. Still, I've got five reminders that I wouldn't be without. They're my life, and I love 'em to bits."

Kay smiled at her sister.

"How do you manage money-wise?"

"Barry sells drugs on the street corner." Lana gave a wink. "No, seriously, their dads pay a share, I get benefits, and I do a little cleaning job when they're all at school. We haven't got much, but we get by."

"John's got all the money in the world, but neither of us are happy." Kay sighed. "He's in love with a bloody ghost, and now I think he's very depressed."

Lana poured hot water into two mugs, threw a tea bag in each, and looked up at Kay with interest as she added a splash of milk.

"In love with a ghost? Come on, don't leave me dangling on a cliff."

Kay shrugged.

"It's a long story, but the crux of the matter is that I told him I didn't want kids. Remember how Mum put us off with all those grisly childbirth reminiscences?"

Lana nodded.

"Yeah, but you can't let Mum's experiences affect *you*. Look at me, I've had five." She flicked one finger in and quickly out of her mouth to make a popping sound. "Easy as shelling peas."

"What about the pain?" Kay took the teabag out of her mug and took a sip. "I mean… how did you cope with it?"

"For the last one I had an epidural. I still had a bit of feeling in my legs, but I didn't feel *any* pain at all. It was the best birthing experience of the lot. Pain relief has moved on from the bit-between-the-teeth-and-bite times."

Kay laughed with her sister and felt a surge of relief.

"I've always dreaded it."

"Nah." Lana shook her head. "Even though their dads have all buggered off, I don't regret having *any* of mine."

***

Kay had never seen fishfingers, peas and chips wolfed down in such a hurry before. Childish chatter ceased as five young people applied themselves to their food.

"They don't get fillet steak, but hey, they're not looking too bad are they?"

Lana stood next to the draining board and nibbled on a stray fishfinger in-between supervising the children's meals and buttering copious slices of doorstep-like bread. Kay enjoyed the brief moment of silence and smiled at Lana, masking a passing stab of envy at her older sister's happiness.

"You're doing a grand job, Sis."

She wondered what any child of hers might look like. *Would it have red hair or take John's darker colouring? Would John in fact still want to consider fathering a child with her?* Ginger or not, she knew one thing; *any kid of hers would be eating fillet steak instead of fishfingers…*

CHAPTER 18 - JOHN

He always kept Robbie's favourite wooden train on top of the toy box *just in case*, and so when he came back from the grave on Christmas Day morning and the train was across the other side of the room, John felt a rising excitement. He pulled back the drawing room curtains, ignoring a layer of dust on the window sills, and put the train back on top of the toy box. By the time he returned after boiling water for a cup of coffee, the train was lying on its side on the carpet.

"Robbie?" John looked around the room. "Come to Daddy!"

The sound of the door knocker was an unwelcome intrusion. John muttered an expletive, made his way to the front of the house, and lifted the latch on the heavy oak door.

"Happy Christmas."

She stood there holding out a present wrapped in gaudy paper. John sighed.

"Sorry, Kay. I haven't bought you anything."

"Can I come in?" Kay stepped over the threshold. "It's cold out there. Oh, I like the candles. Have you done away with the light switch?"

Embers of the previous night's fire glowed in the entrance hall's grate. John threw a log on top of the hot coals, and watched as a tongue of flame licked around the wood.

"I gave Peggy Christmas Day off."

"Are you going to open your present then?" Kay took off her coat. "You'll like it."

He took the gift from her.

"Cheers. You might as well stay for lunch. Peggy left some cold mutton."

"Mutton?"

The way she looked at him was irksome to his spirit. John decided not to reply, and instead led the way to the drawing room.

"It's different in here." Kay shivered. "Why have you changed the carpet and taken the radiator out? Why the candles everywhere? Where's Percy's Venetian blinds?"

John smiled and sat down on the sofa.

"I prefer log fires, candles and curtains. It's cosier." He tore at the wrapping paper. "Baby clothes?"

He stared in puzzlement at the small cardigan and matching bootees, waiting patiently for her reply.

"I suppose it's because I've changed my mind about kids. John, what I'm trying to say is that if you want to give us another chance, then a baby will be fine by me. I've been going to Lana's house and getting to know her brood. She's helped ease my fears about childbirth."

He looked from the tiny clothing to the stranger sitting next to him.

"But I already have a child. I don't need another one. These clothes are too small for him now."

He flinched slightly as she moved in closer and put her hands on his shoulders.

"John. These are clothes for a baby we can have together. A child that's alive. I realise now that I was just frightened of childbirth. I'm thirty six, and now I want to have a baby before I'm too old. Let's get back together and start a family, eh?"

Behind her he saw Robbie's train right itself and chug slowly along towards them.

"I… I don't know." John saw a pudgy hand around the train and then the full solid form of Robbie appeared, followed by Emily. "There would be gossip. Peggy lives in the village, you know."

"Fuck Peggy!" Kay stood up. "I'm offering you something you've always wanted! What's wrong with you?"

John sighed.

"It's a shock, all of a sudden. Let me think about it."

"I'm going upstairs to the en-suite loo." Kay stood up. "We can talk again in a minute."

***

She saw he'd had the hallway re-decorated in her absence. Kay wrinkled her nose at the sight of olive green and white striped wallpaper which now stood in place of Percy's painted plaster. Candle holders adorned the walls, each holding two lighted candles. She shivered and crept up the stairs, which were devoid of the expensive Axminster carpet they had chosen together; instead each step was covered with a kind of hardwearing linoleum.

She decided to have a quick peep into the study. Quietly she opened the door and reached along the wall for the light switch, but the room was already bathed in a glow from some kind of light source she did not recognise sitting atop an old-fashioned writing bureau. An iron bedstead sporting crisp white sheets and a heavy counterpane stood next to a table covered with an ornately embroidered cloth, and on which rested a large porcelain jug and matching round bowl. A tallboy graced the wall nearest the door. She shivered as a cold whoosh of air blew through her and chilled her to the bone.

"What the fuck?"

Kay turned around on hearing footsteps, nearly tripping over her suddenly unfamiliar long cotton dress. John, wearing a black dinner suit complete with frock coat and bow tie, put his arms around her. Robbie clutched at her legs through her floor length skirt. A dark plait of hair fell over her shoulder.

"Welcome home, Emily. I've waited so long for you."

PART THREE

CHAPTER 19 – KAY

He's making love to me, but I know it's *her* that he's thinking of as he lies on top of me just like old times. It's my voice that replies to his words of love, but *her* words that come out of my mouth. She's taken over my body, but thank goodness she cannot invade my mind.

My contraceptive pills are at my flat, and John's ardour increases with every day. There's no way to stop a baby coming. *I don't want to get pregnant this way!* I want it to be *our* baby, but instead he'll see Emily as its mother. I need to get to my flat, but I don't have any control over my body anymore. I'm due a period, but it hasn't come yet. My breasts are unusually sore.

She's made herself at home in this godforsaken rectory, which is now dark and gloomy most of the time. She lights the oil lamps and candles at night, and barks out orders to Peggy. I'm not sure if we're living in the eighteen hundreds or the twentieth century as we hardly ever go outside, and when we do it's only into the garden. John's had all the bathrooms ripped out, and now there's a dirt closet at the back of the house. All the radios and televisions have disappeared too. It's a fucking *mausoleum*!

I feel sorry for Peggy. There's tonnes of labour-saving devices she could use, but she's happy boiling up linens on the Aga, beating rugs on the washing line, or hand washing delicates. I wish I could tell her about our washing machine, which I know John's discarded and put away in the outhouse, but hey, she wouldn't want to use it anyway.

I'm just a fucking disembodied mind! Emily swans around the place like she owns it, ignoring my attempts to guide her to my car, which now doesn't seem to be in the place I last left it. Is it in one of the garages? Who knows? All the computers and landline telephones have gone, including my mobile phone. There doesn't seem to be any way to contact the outside world.

John's happy and has begun writing again. He's set up a desk in one of the spare bedrooms, but he keeps the room locked if he's not using it. From what I can tell by the tradesman that Emily let in, it's got me wondering whether John's had his new study wired up independently from the rest of the house. Tim came around just after Christmas to find out why I'm not at work. John told him we'd split up, and then sent him on his way.

***

Emily's got no bloody idea how to cook. Peggy makes revolting stuff like oxtail broth, pigs' trotters, mutton stew, or liver in a sauce, and the worst…the worst tastes of all are kidneys, brawn, and salt beef. I could *murder* a McDonald's, but Emily eats whatever Peggy leaves out for us, because that's what she's always done. Some of it makes me want to retch.

I'm retching a lot lately, or rather Emily is. There's a baby on its way, I'm certain of it, probably due in the autumn. Emily's sure too, and when John finds out it only seems to make him more passionate and amorous. I'm hoping this pregnancy might mean I get seen by a doctor; hopefully the same one at the GP surgery I went to for the vulval mole. Apparently it's an unusual shape, but thankfully benign. It caused much interest amongst all the other doctors from the surgery when the GP called them in just to look at my bits. I was going to make a quip to bring in all the patients from the waiting room as well, but then decided to keep schtum.

I get tired quite often. Emily plays with Robbie or lies about on the settee if he's having a nap. With no TV, Internet, iPad or phones, and Peggy doing the housework and cooking, there isn't much else to do and it's rather boring. She reads a bit or reads to Robbie, but she cannot seem to concentrate for long. Time drags, and I miss my mobile phone. I miss my sisters too, but I know they won't come looking for me because we were never that close. It's ironic really; I left the estate for a better life, but my sisters are happier even though they don't have much.

I *know* it's not possible to go back in time. I keep thinking of those poor Bronte sisters stuck in that Victorian rectory on the Yorkshire moors with their mad brother. My life's not that dissimilar from theirs now, except that TB isn't so prevalent with the use of antibiotics. John has turned out to be my Branwell, and Emily is…well…Emily Bronte I suppose, but at least they had their writing to keep them occupied. Being around somebody else's two year old all day isn't my idea of fun.

***

My abdomen is protruding now. Lana had scans, midwife appointments and God knows what else. John keeps Emily tucked away inside the rectory. She and Robbie make no effort to go out, and seem to have no inclination to make friends with any of the villagers or their children. I suppose pregnancy in Victorian times was more often than not hushed up, and generally women didn't see a doctor because of the cost. However, John is sitting on *millions*, but obviously doesn't want to spend any of it on Emily's ante-natal care. Perhaps he's doing a Branwell and drinking it all away behind the door of his study.

If only I could get hold of a key…

CHAPTER 20 – JOHN

Who is, or was, Kay? Somebody called Lana, dressed very indecently I might add, is standing in the front porch.

"Hi John. Kay's not at her flat, so I'm wondering whether she's moved back in with you. I've got some baby stuff I want her to have."

The woman is wearing short trousers that end at the middle of her thighs, and some kind of vest with no straps. She looks as though she would be more at home in a brothel.

"You must be mistaken. There is nobody of that name living here."

The woman seems flummoxed, and stares at Emily when she appears next to me.

"But we came to your wedding a few years' back. Don't you remember me? I sure as hell remember *you!*"

This irksome person is a vexation to my spirit. Robbie runs past Emily and holds out his toy train before I can stop him. The woman smiles and bends down to his level.

"Wow! Is that for me? Thank you!"

She takes the train and stares at the boy before standing up to face me.

"Your son?"

"Yes." I indicate with a forefinger in the direction of my own true love. "Mine and Emily's."

"So Kay left you for good, then?"

"There's no Kay living here."

"Fair enough." The woman gives the train back to Robbie. "I'll keep trying her mobile."

She turns away, but she has disturbed my inner peace. Emily's bothered too, and is a bit short with Robbie when he spills a drink. I retreat to my study when the boy becomes somewhat fractious, and wonder about the woman's last remark.

***

Emily always preferred her old bedroom and so of course I was happy to move upstairs, but to be perfectly frank I'm not sure why my desk and sofa had been placed there in the first instance; a lady's bedchamber should not be invaded. It also appears after a recent conversation with Emily that another child is on the way. I must curb my desires now that she is in such a delicate condition.

Meanwhile, I need to ensure the other woman has really gone. However, she is still sitting in a kind of motorised contraption on the driveway, a device in her hand which matches the one inside the middle drawer of my desk. I quickly step up to the desk and unlock the drawer when I hear a tell-tale vibrating sound. Yes, she has sent a message, of which I'm able to read the first line:

'*Kay…where are you?*'

I'm not sure how I've managed to acquire this device, and it unnerves me that I cannot remember. I do not know what to do with it. As it vibrates again I see a picture of me next to a red-headed lady in the background. I'm not wearing my cravat and morning suit, and instead sport short sleeved cotton-type summer wear that bears the inscription '*I'm not a gynaecologist, but I'll have a look*'.

The visage of the auburn-haired beauty is rather appealing. She is dressed in similar shocking garb to that of the woman I have just sent away empty-handed. I am curious as to who she is; so curious in fact that I fear it is time to venture into the village to quench my thirst for this knowledge.

The woman outside has gone. I lock the study door, grab my hat, and creep down the back stairs that are usually only Peggy's domain. I can hear Emily and Robbie's voices somewhere in the house, but far enough away for them not to be aware of what I'm about to do. I close the side door quietly and tiptoe out onto the front gravel path.

The noise hits me at once, suffice to say that I am temporarily overwhelmed. I close my eyes as several more motorised vehicles speed past me in Church Lane. I have not been outside for some time, and when I venture to look again it's as though I've travelled back in time. There I am, standing like a prick in full Victorian garb, complete with stove pipe hat. I must look like Isambard fucking Brunel.

I can see the woman again, coming towards me with Dave Secombe, who's trying not to piss himself laughing.

"Going to a fancy dress party, John?"

My brain is fried and I don't know what's happening to me. The woman speaks.

"My sister Kay is missing. I've just told Officer Secombe, and we were coming back to see you."

Everything seems unreal. Amid my confusion I hold up my wife's phone and point towards the house.

"I can't go back in there. You need to go inside and get her out."

The constable and the woman I now recognise as Lana look at each other. I pass the phone to Dave. Lana comes forward and takes both my hands in hers.

"John, it's Lana. Don't you remember me? Is Kay with you?"

"Yes, I know you." I nod. "Dave needs to go in and bring Emily out here, into Church Lane."

"But where's Kay?" Lana asks with increasing concern. "Has anything happened to her?"

I sigh.

"You wouldn't believe me if I told you. Dave, just go and find Emily… *please*. Trust me. You need to look for Emily."

CHAPTER 21 – KAY

I don't know how I've got here, but I'm being carried along Church Lane towards John by Dave Secombe, whose expression of amazement at the sight of me is making me rather worried. I'm exhausted from fighting, but Dave's too strong for me. I have on some kind of ghastly neck-to-ankle creation, and what's even more confusing I can feel a weird movement in my abdomen. If I didn't know any better I'd say it's similar to how Lana described her first baby kicking many years ago.

John is much thinner, but looks like a well-to-do Victorian gentleman. Dave puts me down and I rush into John's arms. We cling to each other for some time before either one of us speaks.

"People must think we're Victoria and Albert." I wipe tears from my eyes, but I don't know why I'm crying and laughing at the same time. "Remember that photo when Isambard Kingdom Brunel stood in front of those chains? All you need is a fat cigar."

He kisses the top of my head. His heart is hammering against my ear. Passers-by stop and stare. Cars slow down as rubberneckers catch some unexpected entertainment. John's voice comes out as a squeak.

"You look like Miss Muffet after she was frightened by the spider."

"I fucking well don't believe it." Dave looks at John and shakes his head. "It was a bit of a struggle, but I picked up Emily like you said, and…"

"Where's Robbie?" I try and pull myself together. "Did you see a little boy? How about Peggy? She's the cook and cleaner."

Dave suddenly looks rather pale.

"I checked everywhere, but there's nobody else in there. The house looks as though it hasn't been cleaned in months. There's no food in the cupboards except for jars of pickles. The walled garden is overgrown – hasn't been touched maybe since Maggie Cuthbertson died, back in the nineteen sixties."

"We can't walk through that gate ever again." I look over my shoulder at the entrance to our house that was supposed to be our dream home, and grip John's hand with my own as though my life depends on it. "We'll have to go back to my flat, but I don't know where the key is."

John looks at Dave hopefully.

"Your bag is in my study. I hate to have to ask you this, Dave…but would you …er…would you want to make a return trip by any chance?"

Dave looks as though he's about to pass out.

***

The flat is too cramped for the two of us, even though I'm skinner than I've ever been in my life. The GP tells me that I'm undernourished, and he's given me a special diet sheet to follow to make sure the baby is getting some nutrition. It's due at the end of September, and tomorrow I have to go to Brakenrye Hospital for my first scan. I'm nervous about the birth – terrified in fact. Lana tries to soothe my fears, but the closer we get to September the more alarmed I become.

It's hot now. The July sun beats down and I feel heavy and

lethargic. John types away in the flat, trying to get into the habit of writing again. We have royalties coming in from his last screenplay, and so are quite well off. However, it's not money that brings happiness. After all that's happened and what I've got coming, there's really only one place where I want to live. I know it's a run-down council estate, but my four sisters still live there and I find I now want my extended family around me. It's a sore point between us, as John doesn't want to make what he calls a retrograde step.

The rectory stands empty, falling a little bit further into decay with each day that passes (so I'm told). We look to the future now, and the start of our family. We didn't even bother to remove the furniture, because it would mean going back through the front door which neither of us can face at the moment.

***

I lie on Julie the midwife's couch. Cold gel is placed on my swollen abdomen, and Julie runs the ultrasound probe over the gel.

"There's a strong heartbeat, and I can see the sex of the baby if you would like to know?"

I look hopefully towards John, who grins and nods.

"Yes, okay." I reply. "I think it's a girl. Am I right?"

"You certainly are." Julie smiles at me. "She's looking very healthy, and so are you if I may say so. You've managed to get back up to a normal weight now."

"I feel fine." I reply.

"We'll just increase your ante-natal appointments as you're getting nearer your due date, but I don't think we'll bother with another scan. I'll do blood pressure, urine and blood tests today, but I don't have any concerns about you at all."

I feel mightily relieved as John and I drive back to the flat.

CHAPTER 22 – JOHN

Just to keep the peace I give in and buy one of the run-down maisonettes off the council that nobody wants on the Broadberry estate. I can't believe Kay wants to go back. I'm a fucking millionaire for Christ's sake, but I can see she's happier amongst her sisters. I got some painters and decorators in quick, because the baby's due any time now. At least our place now looks better than any of the others in the street.

The four sisters are like mother hens, all clucking around Kay all day. I shut myself away and type in the spare bedroom and let the madness go on all around me. Cassie's voice has a foghorn-like penetration, Miranda's forever cleaning and plumping up the cushions after Kay stands up, Louie and Lana have enough kids between them to start a school of their own, but at least my wife is happy again.

We sit contentedly in our pocket handkerchief-sized garden one evening in the middle of September. The summer heat is beginning to die down. Kay knits frantically as though our daughter's life depends on it. I clear my throat.

"You know I had no control over my actions regarding Emily, don't you?"

The needles stop clacking for a moment.

"Let's not go there. She took over both of our lives, but hey, we're free of her now."

The knitting continues apace, and I risk a bollocking.

"I think the rectory's suffused with malevolent spirits from the past, angry that they're dead and we're still alive. What do you think?"

"Sounds plausible." Kay shrugs, and I carry on.

"Do you know, I asked around in the village about Peggy but nobody knew anything about her, but there was one old boy who'd heard his grandmother talk about a Peggy who had lived next door to them and had worked at the rectory in Reverend Cuthbertson's time."

Kay looks up from reading the pattern.

"Oh?"

"Yeah. I found her grave in Southcombe churchyard. She died in eighteen seventy."

***

It's the sound of police sirens that wakes our daughter up and makes her decide to begin her entrance into this unforgiving world. At three thirty on the morning of September 23rd, I am nudged awake in an unpleasantly damp bed.

"The waters broke a short while ago, John." Kay struggles to climb out. "I'm getting pains now. I think I'd better get dressed."

I'm suddenly filled with excitement. Our daughter is on her way! I quickly throw on some jeans and a jumper and grab the case that Kay has so carefully packed. Kay puts on one of her tent-like maternity dresses, and I wrap my arms around her.

"I love the way you look now."

She rolls her eyes at me.

"Oh yeah, I must look a bloody sight." Her face creases

momentarily. "Ouch. That was a contraction, I think."

"One less to worry about. "I try and offer some kind of aid. "When there's none left our daughter will be here. To take your mind off when the next one's coming, let's try and finally decide on her name."

"I can't think straight at the moment."

She clutches her abdomen, and I feel somewhat useless because there's nothing I can do for her.

"Time for some coffee before we go?" I suggest hopefully.

She shakes her head.

"I just want to get to the hospital."

***

Not even the birds are chirping their dawn chorus just yet. A fine mist rolls over the concrete jungle as we leave the estate. Kay frantically texts her sisters in-between clutching at her stomach.

"I wish Mum was still alive."

I turn towards her momentarily.

"I'm sure she's looking down on you."

There's a snort from the front seat.

"You must be joking. She always said that once you were dead, then you were dead, good and proper."

I drive as slowly as I can so as not to cause her any discomfort. There's hardly any traffic about anyway, and we reach Brackenrye Hospital at 04:10. A solitary receptionist on duty in the maternity unit yawns and looks to me as though she ought to be in bed. Kay groans from her wheelchair, leans forward and wraps her arms around her middle. I face the receptionist and try to keep the breathlessness out of my voice.

"Kay Finbow. She's been having contractions for about an hour I think."

"Have the waters broken?"

"Yes!" Kay shouts and winces. "Please don't send me home again!"

The receptionist smiles and walks around the counter to face us.

"Follow me and I'll show you to your room."

It's not quite home from home, but it's pleasant enough. There's a high hospital bed, a duvet to match the curtains, and a large bath in an adjoining wet room for water births. A midwife pops her head around the door.

"Hi. I'm Annemarie. I'll grab some admission forms and I'll be with you in two ticks."

***

I'm banished to the waiting room whilst Kay is examined. On the wall is a frieze of smiling new mothers and sleeping infants. I cannot wait to see my own child; I've dreamed about this moment for so long. I'm beginning to think Robbie was a hallucination due to the fact that I've been as broody as a mother hen for at least five years.

I'm called back in with the news that Kay is already three centimetres dilated. After another hour she asks for a mobile epidural, and so the midwife pages the on-call anaesthetist. I hate to see my wife in pain. She looks terrified. I grab her hand.

"It's a good pain, my love. It means our baby is on her way."

"It's alright for you." Kay grimaces. "It doesn't feel very good to me."

I am edgy until the anaesthetist arrives to put Kay out of her misery. He looks half asleep, and his hair sticks up at an angle on one side. Again I am ejected from the room, but return to find a smiling wife sitting up on the bed.

"This stuff's awesome!" She grins. "Let's decide on a name now."

"What about Emmeline?" I venture. "I like that one."

Kay wrinkles her nose.

"It reminds me too much of you-know-who. No, I like Mia. Short and sweet."

At this moment in time I'm happy to grant her anything she desires. After months of wrangling, I concede.

"Mia Victoria?"

"Lovely!" Kay leans over to give me a kiss. "I wish she'd hurry up though."

"I love you." I return the kiss. "You're doing fine."

I settle down next to her, and prepare for a long wait.

***

"Push!" Annemarie has a quick look down the business end. "The head's coming!"

I feel like crying, but don't want to embarrass myself in front of the nursing staff. I slide my arm around Kay's back as she grabs both knees with her hands.

"I can't feel much." Kay complains. "I don't know if I'm doing it right."

Annemarie waves away her fears.

"Just push as though you're emptying your bowels. It won't be long now."

My wife has turned into a warrior, pushing and grunting with all her might. Sweat pours off all of us in the confines of the room. I move down to stand by Annemarie. With every push I can see the top of Mia's head presenting and then retracting.

"Come on!" I shout. "Push as hard as you can!"

I think Kay has gone into another world. She looks straight ahead but doesn't see me as she strains in what I can only describe as a bestial way. A crown of dark hair emerges, soon followed by the shoulders and the rest of my daughter. Annemarie expertly wraps Mia in a towel and gives her to me.

"Cut the cord and then give her to Mum."

It's the first time I get to see my baby's face, and she's awake. Emily's blue eyes stare at me amongst the vernix and the blood. Aghast, I'm struck dumb as I stare at my lover's features. I cut the cord with tears rolling down my cheeks.

"Don't worry." Annemarie laughs. "Many dads cry at the sight of their firstborn."

With shaking hands I place the baby in Kay's arms, who looks down at her and screams.

CHAPTER 23 – KAY

It's coming up to midnight. My sisters have been and gone, and made more cooing noises than a flock of bloody doves. John has given in to sleep, and I sit in a rocking chair in our nursery with this *thing …Emily …* sucking at my breasts. I don't even want to look at its face; those blue eyes do not belong to either me or John.

The midwife says I've got the *baby blues*, but she doesn't know the half of it. I have grown another woman's child in my womb; a child that should never have been born in the first place. I see a terrible similarity to my situation and that of Rosemary Woodhouse, Ira Levin's character who carries the devil's spawn.

It stares and sucks, and sucks and stares. I am mesmerised by its eyes. It never seems to sleep, but it doesn't cry. Lana and Louie tell me I don't realise how lucky I am. Lucky? I think I'm the *unluckiest* new mother ever.

John is over the moon of course. He gazes at it like a sick pig. Neither of us have mentioned Emily's name since that terrible day in the delivery room, but this baby is a constant reminder of his infidelity.

My milk is this thing's life force. I remember how I'd told John several times that I didn't want a baby, and how I wish I'd stuck to my guns. However, was I actually *present* at conception? *I don't think so.*

What's the point of blurting all this out to the midwife? They'll send for the men in white coats if I tell her what really happened. Anyway, the health visitor will be coming tomorrow instead, as today was the last time the midwife had to visit. Apparently I'm doing well, but all I can say is I'm doing a good job of holding it all together. I haven't 'lost' it yet, but I don't think it'll be long before I do.

****

John stirs as I climb back into bed.

"Is she asleep?"

"No." I reply. "She's just lying in the cot and staring at the mobile."

I have to remember the correct pronoun when John's about.

****

As it grows and becomes more aware, it stares at things I cannot see. Its eyes quite frequently follow an unseen presence across the room, and always at the same time the cat will dive for cover. I spend more and more time with my sisters, anything to get out of the house. I leave John to his writing and plonk the baby in its buggy, who doesn't settle as well as in its own place. Maybe the noise of all the kids gets on its nerves. I'm not that enamoured with the din either, but somehow I feel safe.

I realise that I just cannot bond with this infant; I don't even like it. The way it looks at me unnerves me down to my socks. It never cries, but it seldom laughs either. The cobalt eyes just watch and wait … for what I don't know.

It starts to chatter at eighteen months, and always when I stand outside its bedroom I hear it talking away to itself. However, one morning when I hear it say *"Hello Mummy"* and I'm not even in the room, a cold shiver runs through me. I feel it's time to let the devoted daddy know just what's going on. I wait until we're lying in bed in post-coital bliss one Sunday night with my head on his shoulder.

"John, there's something you ought to know."

I slide one leg across his thighs and rest my right arm on his chest.

"What?"

He's sleepy, and I must drop the bomb before he dozes off.

"I think Emily is back."

He throws me off and sits up.

"What do you mean?"

"It's Mia. She…she can see her I'm sure. If I wait outside her room in the mornings I hear her speaking and saying *Mummy*."

"Perhaps she's calling *you*?" John suggests, giving me a strange look."

"No." I shake my head. "She just endures me, because she's dependent. I'm sure when she's up and running I'll be yesterday's news."

"I didn't know any of this." John sighs. "You should have said something before."

I cannot help the words, which now tumble and fall.

"She was trying to say *Robbie* the other day, I'm sure of it. John, she gives me the creeps. Our own daughter, and she gives me the fucking *creeps!*"

There. I've said it. I feel better for the rant though. John puts an arm around me.

"I've not seen Emily since… well… you know. I'm sure if she *was* back I'd be aware of her."

"Perhaps she's just come back for her child." My eyes fill with tears. "It's a terrible thing to say, but I feel nothing for that baby …nothing at all."

John gives me a squeeze.

"You need help, love. What d'you say about coming to see the GP with me?"

"I'm not going to take any anti-depressants, so it'll be a waste of time." I pull away from him. "Again, it's Emily who's causing all this trouble."

John lies back against the pillows.

"Post-natal depression can affect any woman. It's nothing to be ashamed of."

I leap out of bed and face him, hot tears in my eyes and angrier than I've been in a long while.

"Don't patronise me! The bloody kid is not normal! You wear blinkers as far as she's concerned…I've seen enough of my sisters' children recently to realise there's something wrong with her!"

"Okay, okay." John holds up his hands in supplication. "You win. I'll send off my screenplay at the end of the week, and then I'll take some time off to help you with Mia."

"Thank you." I let out a sigh of relief. "You'll soon see what I mean."

CHAPTER 24 – JOHN

I miss Kay, but I know I can visit her any time as she's only a few streets away on the estate staying with Louie for a fortnight's break. I have Mia to myself for now, and she really is the most delightful little girl. She likes being read to and giggles at Seuss's *Cat in the Hat* stories. She knows she'll get chocolate button sandwiches for tea if she manages to eat all her dinner, and I don't have any trouble trying her with new foods. She sleeps soundly at night, and seems altogether much more relaxed and chatty with me than she does with Kay.

I wheel her about in the buggy, but the area's a bit rough and the swings and slide have been vandalised. I know there's a nice park at Southcombe, and one autumn day in October I decide to take Mia to the kiddies' playground there because I have a secret yearning to visit the old rectory again. It still hasn't been sold, even though I've dropped the price. Maybe we didn't know at the time what everybody else seems to.

I strap Mia in her car seat and we head on over to the park. She's impatient to play, and runs directly to the sandpit. I'm the only man in the vicinity, and the clique of mothers regard me with suspicion. I keep my focus on Mia, and try not to look like Billy-no-mates as I sit there and watch her build sandcastles.

I've remembered to bring her something to eat, and at lunch time we munch contentedly before we stroll hand-in-hand towards the rectory. As we enter Church Lane, Mia suddenly tugs at my hand and pulls me in the direction of the graveyard. Puzzled, I let her lead me.

"Daddy! There!"

She points with a pudgy finger towards the back of the churchyard, and my blood runs cold. I let go of her hand and follow her as she runs along the path by the side of the church. To my horror she makes straight for Emily's grave and plonks her little body upon it.

"Mummy." She nods thoughtfully. "Mummy and Robbie."

I'm too gobsmacked to think about setting foot inside the rectory. We sit there on Emily's grave and look at one another. Mia smiles at me and places a crumpled dandelion on the mossy earth in front of the tombstone that she's picked up from somewhere. The dandelion is falling apart; a bit like me really, especially when I spy Maxwell Grant's grave a few metres along from Emily's as I survey my surroundings. I realise he's been pruning and planting phantom fruit trees one hundred and twenty odd years after he'd been laid in the earth himself.

***

Kay is due back this morning and I'm not sure whether to tell her she was right all along, or to say nothing and hope it'll all go away. I plump for the latter and welcome my wife with open arms as she runs in through the door. I pull her towards me with one hand while carrying Mia with the other.

"We've missed you!"

"I've had a great time." Kay grins at me. "But I'm glad to be home."

The three of us have a little cuddle, but all too soon I can tell that

Mia has grown rather silent. At lunch time she's fussing over her food again, causing Kay's mouth to pucker in annoyance. Kay looks up at me and I feel a bollocking coming on.

"Have you been feeding her shit food?"

"No, of course not." I pray to God that the dustmen have been. "She's been fine while you've been away… really."

"Ha, well… it must be *me* then." Kay sighs. "Mia, please eat your lunch."

"No."

I'm amazed at the accompanying expression of venom. Kay and Mia glare at each other like two prize fighters. Mia's lip quivers, and she's the first one to give in.

"Don't want *you*. Want Mummy."

The deathly pallor on Kay's face can be likened to a corpse. Mia turns to her left, holds out her arms, and looks in the direction of the clock on the wall.

"Mummy!"

The hands on the kitchen clock suddenly begin to rotate at a terrifying speed. Mia chuckles and throws her plate on the floor. Kay's struck dumb with her mouth open, but I need to establish some kind of control. I yank Mia out of her high chair and gently smack her wrist.

"Naughty girl! Now you can wait until dinner time!"

The wailing starts, while the clock's hands fall to half past six and stay there. I plonk Mia in front of the electronic babysitter, and she is soon enjoying her favourite programme on CBeebies. I stumble back into the kitchen where Kay still isn't moving. Aghast, she looks up at me.

"What the hell happened there?"

"Mia had a paddy."

"Don't avoid the issue, John." Kay glances up at the clock. "Do you or do you not agree that Emily's ghost has followed us here?"

I try and give her some hope to cling to.

"We're outside the rectory and so I don't think she can do much. However, it's obvious that Mia can see her, and probably Robbie as well. You were right. I'm sorry I didn't believe you."

I hate owning up to being such a prick, but by the beam on Kay's face I know she's happy I've done it.

"You don't know what that means to me." She comes around the table and gives me a kiss. "I thought I was going mad."

We cling together while the remains of Mia's spaghetti Bolognese lie all around our feet.

CHAPTER 25 – KAY

I cannot sleep at night at the thought that *she's* watching us. I wish to God we'd never moved into that bloody rectory. One day soon after the clock incident while *it* naps and John starts a new screenplay, I search on Google for old newspaper cuttings from the Southcombe Standard featuring the word '*Cuthbertson*'. I'm surprised at the amount of information that's available online.

In the obituaries from December 1866 there's a grainy picture of a very stern-looking vicar and a woman who I assume is his widow. Delia Cuthbertson, dressed in black bombazine and a rather queenly black lace mantilla, mourns the death of the Reverend Arthur Cuthbertson, who has passed after a short illness leaving behind a grieving widow and 8 sons and daughters.

The children's names are listed, and I realise I'm looking at Emily's parents. The two unsmiling faces give no clues to their life at the rectory in the 1800s. Emily's name is given last, which leads me to assume she had been the youngest of the brood and was therefore expected to become a companion to Delia in her time of grief.

I find a *Hatches, Matches and Dispatches* bit dated April 17th 1868. The funeral of Emily Maud, daughter of the late Reverend Arthur Cuthbertson, had taken place in the church. I read that apparently Emily had succumbed to a fever five days before. There's another

Cuthbertson funeral mentioned later that year, when I read that Delia died of a broken heart.

Later editions show a young man, the Reverend Lionel Cuthbertson, looking not unlike Arthur. In 1873 he marries a Charlotte Lucy Fielding, who eventually produces a son, William, and two daughters, Edwina and Elizabeth.

There are many Cuthbertson obituaries over successive editions, and I read how William eventually takes over as rector from his father. The last of the incumbents, Margaret Maud, a spinster granddaughter of William, apparently lived at the rectory in solitary splendour for many years before succumbing to cancer in 1965.

***

It occurs to me why there might be no buyers for the rectory, and I mention my thoughts to John one evening after dinner.

"We need to get the house re-wired. There's no electricity. A few bathrooms wouldn't go amiss either. You got the builders to rip them all out, if you remember. We'll get much more money for it."

He gives a *tut* of annoyance.

"No I don't remember doing any of it. I just want to get rid of the bloody place now. I want us to move forward together and put all this behind us."

I tentatively persist.

"So … shall I get some quotes then?"

I'm relieved when he gives a nod.

"I'll get the builders in who I used last time. They'll think I'm a total dipshit though."

"Let them think what they like." I give him a hug. "They haven't got a clue what's happened to us."

He seems somehow ashamed of his actions, but it's easy to forgive somebody who appears so contrite. We've been tiptoeing around each other and trying not to mention Emily's name for quite a few weeks now in the run-up to Christmas. I don't know how it's going to affect him now he'll have to go back to that rectory and instruct the builders. He must stay strong and not let Emily overpower him again.

****

I feel safe in the bosom of my family on Christmas Day. I don't care that I'm doing all the cooking this year, because there's enough of us to fill the house and make Emily feel unwelcome. Mia runs around with her cousins, and I even get a few smiles out of her when she opens her presents. We've spoiled her rotten and she's happy enough playing with her new toys.

I never thought I'd get 16 of us seated for dinner, but I manage to after John, Barry and Frankie take most of the furniture out of the dining room and put it in the garage. I sit there like Queen Bee and preside over Lana with her five, Louie with her three boys, Cassie with little Jackie, and Katy with Thomas and Billy. Just before John carves the enormous turkey we all hold hands around the table and instead of saying Grace we sing 'We Wish You a Merry Christmas', which little Jackie has been brainwashing her mother with after learning it at nursery. Singing with the family chokes me up, and I wonder why the hell I've been estranged from my sisters for so long.

Our mum should be with us at Christmas, but doubtless she's in a happier place. It's as though the same thought has touched all four of my siblings, as when I look up they're all wiping tears from their eyes as well.

CHAPTER 26 – JOHN

It's a bleak morning in early January when I turn into Church Lane and pull up outside the iron gates of the rectory. I have no desire to enter the grounds until the builders arrive, and so I back up to the gates and sit there. After about fifteen minutes a white van speeds along the lane and pulls up next to me.

"Sorry we're on the drag, mate." Steve Addison jumps out and shakes my hand. "Boz had to stop for a crap."

Boz looks suitably sheepish as he steps out of the car.

"How's it going, John?"

I shake Boz's hand and hope he's washed it. I wonder if I'm prepared for the amount of mickey-taking I'm about to receive.

"Nice to meet up again, guys." I unlock the gates. "Park up by the front door and lock the car and follow you in."

Steve nods and climbs back into the driver's seat, while Boz walks through the gate, his hobnailed boots crunching on the gravel. Steve starts the van's engine again, then rolls down the window and sticks his head out.

"So… what do you want us to do?"

"Er… it'll be re-fitting three bathrooms and the en-suite shower room, and then re-wiring the whole house."

"Christ." Steve whistles softly under his breath. "We already did that, mate, and then took it all out again.”

“Don’t go there.” I sigh. “Just take the money and do your job.”

Steve rolls the van slowly up the driveway, and with great reluctance I activate the central locking and follow him. The first thing I notice is Maxwell Grant training fruit tree branches along the boundary walls amongst the overgrown brambles of many summers. My heart skips a beat, but thankfully Steve and Boz seem none the wiser.

Max waves to me and I resist the urge to raise my hand in acknowledgement. I unlock the front door, and fish on the left for the light switch, which of course isn’t there.

“Look guys, I think I can leave you to it. You’re familiar with the house anyway. What about me giving you the key, and you can come and go as you please? Just do the same as you did last time.”

I’m anxious to get away, but Steve has other ideas.

“Where’s the khasi, mate? Have we got to order a Portaloo?”

“I’ll show you. It’s round the back. The side gate is locked, and so we’ll have to go through the house.”

Steve shrugs and they follow me into the hallway and along the back corridor that leads to the kitchen. Robbie runs towards me. He’s grown in the intervening months, and if I could put a photo of myself aged 3 next to him, it would show an uncanny similarity.

“Daddy!” Robbie takes hold of my hand “You’re home!”

I panic and wrench my hand away from the boy. Steve shoots me a puzzled look.

“You alright mate?”

Emily appears, clad in a long gown of midnight blue velvet. Her arms reach out to me and I close my eyes to shut out the sight of her mouth opening to speak.

“I want Mia!”

I turn in Steve’s direction and nod.

"I'm just a bit dizzy. If you unlock the back door, the toilet will be to the left of the patio in what looks like a shed."

"Fuck me, you're as white a sheet!" Boz steadies me with one arm. "We'll take it from here. You go and sit in the car for a minute."

I allow Boz to help me to the door, and then walk as quickly as I can to the safety of my car parked on the other side of the gate. I look through the rear-view mirror, and with some degree of horror see Emily and Robbie running towards the car. I start the engine and screech away as fast as ever I can.

***

Kay and Mia are playing with the building bricks when I get home. I'm still shaky, and flop down onto the settee.

"You're making the old man noise." Kay grins at me. "You mustn't make that sound when you sit down."

"Sorry."

I give her a thin smile. She seems happier since Christmas. Emily has kept her distance. I hate to burst her bubble, but Kay needs to be on her guard. I'll wait until Mia is asleep tonight, and then tell her what she doesn't want to hear.

CHAPTER 27 – KAY

I think I may be getting through to Mia. She's still enthralled with her Christmas presents even three weeks into January. She lets me sit and play with her, instead of pushing me away and calling for Emily. She focuses on *me*, instead of looking at an invisible entity. We've had no visitations as far as I can tell, and the kitchen clock tells the correct time again.

John tells me to watch Mia like a hawk. I know he's concerned that Emily might come back, but I told him my opinion; if he's not openly encouraging her presence and strengthening the bond between them by touching her and calling out for her, then the energy between them will be weak.

John and I are getting on better than ever. In fact, I think I may even be pregnant again as I've missed a period, which is unusual for me. I'll leave Mia with John next week and take a urine sample to the GP. He might want to examine me, and it's better if Mia isn't running around at the same time. It's a good thing I'm not really ill, as doctors' appointments seem as rare as rocking horse shit these days.

I finally see why women want babies. When there's a reaction from the infant and you feel as if it actually likes you, then you cannot help but bond with it. Mia follows me around now, and while not openly loving, she has lots of smiles for me and is becoming rather delightful. She hasn't yet called me '*Mummy*', but I'm ever hopeful, and John is ecstatic with the upturn in our family dynamics; he's writing like there's no tomorrow. Royalties are still flooding in, and he talks of moving to a bigger house. However, I feel safe here with my sisters, who are always popping in.

I feel guilty that I kept calling Mia '*it*'. She didn't ask to be born, and she's only a tot.

***

Mia and I are tagging along with Cassie and Jackie today at the swimming pool; I'd never even thought of mothers and toddlers' swimming lessons before. I'd always felt closer to Lana, but now see Cassie more as Jackie is only a few months older than Mia, and the girls are already firm friends.

I look over my shoulder at their little faces in the back seat of my car, but can see no cousin-like similarity in their features. Jackie has our red hair, pale skin and green eyes. Mia's tresses are dark brown. She has bright blue eyes, and looks the image of Emily.

"They're getting big." Cassie follows my gaze. "Time's going by so quickly".

I grin at my sister.

"Two little beauties. Don't let on, but I think I may be pregnant again."

"Wow! So soon!" Cassie laughs. "Wasn't there anything on T.V?"

We giggle together as I pull away from the kerb.

"Yeah. You know… that One Born Every Minute programme."

It's a ten minute drive to the leisure centre. We pry the girls out of the car seats and grab our bags from the boot.

"Are you signing up for the whole course?" Cassie expertly settles Jackie on her hip. "It'll finish at Easter, I think."

I nod, pleased at the opportunity.

"Sure. I don't know where I'd be without the four of you. I've come to motherhood a bit late in life."

"It's a constant learning curve." Cassie rolls her eyes. "I'm still in discovery mode as well."

***

Mia hangs on to me for dear life as I climb gingerly into the water, accompanied by a cacophony from 15 other protesting toddlers. I stroke her hair.

"It's okay. Mummy's here."

Two little arms slide around my neck.

"Mummy."

I'm chuffed to bits. I squeeze my daughter and kiss her cheek.

"We're going to have fun today. See this rubber ring?" I pull a yellow duck-shaped floating aid towards me. "Mummy will put you inside it, but will hold on to you as well, so don't worry."

Jackie is happily splashing about in her rubber ring, but Mia is having none of it, and her wailing increases with each of my feeble attempts to disentangle her from my hip.

"It's only her first time." Cassie spins Jackie around slowly in the water. "She'll get used to it."

I don't mind Mia's unwillingness to participate. I'm enjoying being needed. It's the first time I've made any headway, and I'm savouring every moment.

CHAPTER 28 – JOHN

Steve and Boz are getting on my tits. It seems as though every five minutes there's another call. I'm happily building Duplo houses with Mia when my mobile vibrates yet again.

"What?"

I cannot keep the irritation out of my voice, but Steve catches on very quickly.

"Sorry mate, but Boz has walked out. I just need a hand with getting the last bath upstairs. I can't do that one on me own."

I sigh

"Why's the fucker walked off?"

Mia looks at me and smiles.

"Fucker."

I cover the mouthpiece, stare at Mia and whisper.

"No. That's a naughty word. Daddy won't say it again."

Mia throws a Duplo brick at me, and I grin.

"I'll have to bring Mia with me. Kay's popped out for a while."

"It won't take long." The relief in Steve's voice is audible. "Ten minutes at the most, mate. I can do the rest meself."

***

I purposely leave the car outside the rectory gates, and disregard Max as he trains fruit tree branches along the boundary walls. However, with Mia clamped to my hip I soon realise it's not going to be as easy this time to ignore the ghosts of gardeners past as I walk towards the front door. I reach in my pocket for something to distract me; in my haste I realise I've left my phone at home.

"Max!" Mia shrieks. "Hello!"

I walk a bit faster and push open the door. Peggy stands there to greet us.

"Welcome home, Mr John."

She holds out her arms to take my daughter. I squeeze Mia more tightly towards me and walk straight through Peggy whilst waving at Steve with my free hand.

"I hope this isn't going to take too long."

"Nah, mate." Steve shrugs. "Boz got the willies and stormed off, but I can't work out what he's on about."

"What's wrong with the wanker?"

Too late, I've forgotten that Mia's not a baby anymore.

"Wanker." Mia chuckles. "Wanker."

Emily and Robbie look over the balcony at us from the mezzanine floor. I grip Mia like my life depends on it.

"Mummy!" Mia points up in Emily's direction. "My mummy!"

I watch Steve's face change to a deathly puce. I already know why Boz has had an attack of the willies.

"What's she looking at?" Steve follows Mia's gaze. "Boz saw a woman with long brown hair in the en-suite bathroom."

I shrug as nonchalantly as possible.

"He's probably imagining it."

Meanwhile Mia's going ape-shit trying to wriggle away and get to Emily. I hold her in a vice-like grip, and she starts to howl.

"Shh!" I whisper in her ear. "We can go home soon."

"Am home." Mia sobs. "With Mummy."

I need to get back to the car as soon as possible. The bath sits in a corner of the hallway, but I need to put Mia down in order to carry one end of it. A lightbulb moment strikes. I whisper to Mia.

"Sit in the bath, and Daddy will give you a ride upstairs.

Distracted, Mia's tears stop momentarily. Emily and Robbie disappear from the balcony to my great relief. Mia lies supine on the bottom of the bath as I walk around to one end of it and look at Steve.

"Ready?"

"Yeah." Steve picks up the other end. "One, two, three…lift!"

The bloody thing is heavy and wobbles about. Alarmed, Mia jumps up and starts to climb out.

"No, no." I shake my head. "Sit still!"

She begins to scream whilst trying to escape her confines. I put my end down and lift her out.

"Sit there on the bottom step and watch Daddy. I'll help Steve take the bath upstairs and then we'll go back to the car."

My heart's hammering in my chest. For once Mia does as she's told and sits silently watching us. I virtually run up the stairs holding on to the bath, trying to see where Emily has gone. I look behind. Mia's still sitting on the step.

"Hang on!" Steve grumbles. "I can't go backwards that fast!"

After an eternity we reach the bathroom and I let my burden fall.

"Okay mate?" I nod at Steve. "I'll be off now."

I don't even wait for his reply. I race downstairs, ready to grab Mia and run.

She has gone.

***

I dash around like a thing possessed.

"Mia!" I shout into empty rooms. "Mia!"

Steve runs downstairs, concerned at the commotion.

"What's happened, mate?"

"Mia's missing." I check the front door, which is still closed. "She must be in here somewhere."

"I'll look out the back." Steve brushes past me down the corridor. "We'll find her."

I know she did not go up the stairs behind me, and so I race around the downstairs reception rooms, the kitchen, dining room, cloakroom and conservatory again.

Nothing.

Steve returns empty handed from the grounds.

"The back door was locked. She couldn't have got out there anyway."

"Cheers." I try and keep the panic out of my voice. "Just carry on with what you were doing. She's probably just wandered off somewhere."

I take the stairs three at a time to the mezzanine floor. Our old bedroom and my study are empty. I continue up to the third floor and kick open the bedroom doors, hating myself for leaving Mia unattended even for five minutes. On the top floor landing I stop in my tracks, breathless, at the sight of Robbie.

"Hello Daddy."

I'm momentarily at a loss for words. We stand staring at each other until my breathing calms.

"Where's Mia?"

"Mummy's got her. She's fine." Robbie smiles at me. "She told me to tell you not to bother looking for her, because you'll never find her now."

He disappears into thin air in the blink of an eye. I'm alone, left standing like a prize prat outside the nursery – a nursery which would never know any of my children.

CHAPTER 29 – KAY

I keep hugging myself, and I can't wait for John to come home. He hasn't left a note, and his mobile phone is on the floor in the front room next to Mia's bricks. I expect he's taken Mia to the park for a bit of fresh air.

I start to get worried when I've cooked dinner and it's dark, but they're still not home. His car has gone, and so he could be anywhere.

When the phone rings, I pick it up but do not recognise the mobile number.

"Hello?"

"Mrs Finbow, it's Steve."

"What's up, Steve? Is John with you?"

"Yes. I'll put him on. I'll leave you two to talk in peace."

The relief I feel at knowing they're okay is short lived.

"Kay?"

John doesn't sound right. I begin to panic.

"What's wrong? Is Mia okay?"

I hear a sigh before he continues, and my blood runs cold.

"We're at the rectory. Mia disappeared. I had to help Steve carry a bath upstairs and I put her down for just five minutes, I swear. Emily's got her, Kay. Robbie came and told me."

My legs turn to jelly, and I sink down onto the nearest chair. I can't think straight.

"Have you phoned the police? Why wasn't Boz there?"

"I have, but you know as well as I do it'll do no good." John's voice sounds terrifyingly matter-of-fact. "We've been searching the house with the police for hours, even out in the garden, although the front and back doors were shut. She's *gone*, Kay. Boz had already seen Emily and legged it. I don't blame him. You can't come to the house – you *know* that, don't you."

I know it only too well. I cry as the grim knowledge of Mia's whereabouts overpowers me, causing my voice to shake and my heart to sink.

"I bet there's one place you haven't searched … ". I hiccup.

"Where?"

I hear an upturn in his tone.

"The churchyard … oh God…" I sob. "But don't let her be there…"

His voice comes over at once, authoritative and in command.

"I'll go there right now. You stay put."

***

There's no way I can remain at home. John's car is still outside the rectory gates as I speed past on my way to the churchyard. I have to park the car quite a way down the lane due to two police cars and an ambulance which have pulled up and are taking up space alongside the church wall. My heart thuds noisily in my chest at the sight of them.

I grab Mia's favourite dolly from the back seat and begin to run. A cold January mist has rolled in and I'm sweating, but chilled to the bone. There's a gathering of officials and paramedics at the end of the path that runs along the side of the church. I push through the melee, frantic and running on auto-pilot.

"I'm Mia's mother!"

John leaps at me and pushes me back.

"No!" His eyes are streaming with tears. "Don't come any further!"

"Let me go!" I scream at him. "I want to be with Mia! She needs me!"

With a superhuman effort I wrench myself away from him and stumble my way forwards. John shouts a warning before running after me.

"Don't touch her! Forensics are on their way!"

The crowd part slightly, which enables me to see Mia, white-faced in rigor mortis, lying on her back on top of Emily's grave, with her arms folded neatly across her chest.

"Dear God!" I drop to my knees beside her. "Who could have done this?"

But in my heart of hearts I *know*.

The crowd are silent. I lay Mia's dolly next to her little body, and let my salty tears drip onto the cold, hard earth.

***

I leave my car at the church and John drives me home, as I cannot seem to function properly. The wobbly tower of bricks that Mia had constructed still stands on the carpet next to John's phone when we walk into the front room together, holding on to each other for support.

We crash down into the soft folds of the sofa, and I bury my head in John's chest and let another river of tears soak into the fabric of his jacket.

"She's got what she wants." I sob. "Let's hope she doesn't want *you* as well to make her family complete."

John holds me tightly and we cry together. I've never seen him weep in all the years we've been together.

"I'm never going back to that house. I don't care if Steve calls me fifty times a day. I shall never set foot in that place again. I don't think I was ever supposed to be a father – well, not to living kids anyway."

The news that I'd been so excited to impart only a few hours' ago comes to the forefront of my frazzled brain. All I want to do now is to end his feeling of hopelessness.

"I'm pregnant, John." I kiss away his tears. "The GP had the results back today from my urine test. This one is definitely *ours.*"

Now I don't know whether he's crying because of Mia, or because of my statement. Maybe it's a bit of both.

CHAPTER 30 – ETHAN FINBOW
APRIL 2018

I don't know why Mum and Dad only ever had one child – me. I mean… it's not as though they could never afford to have more; Dad's a multi-millionaire for God's sake. I would have liked a brother or sister, but I suppose they're getting on a bit for having babies. They probably don't even have sex now anyway.

I must be the only kid at my private school who lives on a council estate. It's grim. I dare not ask anybody back for tea after lessons. Mum doesn't want to move because her sisters all live within a stone's throw of our rabbit hutch. We've got a summer house on the French Riviera and Dad's offered to buy my aunts bigger places, but they're all happy living on this poxy Broadberry Estate. Every time I walk to the fish and chip shop I get asked if I want to buy drugs by the moron who stands on the street corner.

Dad once showed me where they used to live at Southcombe Rectory. We sat in the car outside on the road, but never went in. Why the hell won't they move back there? They still own it. It was on the market for years, but nobody ever bought it. I told them recently that in 6 months' time when 18 I'm going to live there and have the place done up, but Dad had an epi and told me he'd never pay a penny towards its upkeep. Therefore when I leave school in July I'm going to have a gap year before Uni and get myself a job, move into the rectory, and live how I should have been living all these years.

Dad said he'd buy me a car for my birthday if I don't move into the rectory. He might be as rich as Croesus, but he can't control me once I turn 18. I'll get myself a job filling shelves at the supermarket … anything, I don't care what I do; but by hook or by crook I'm going to branch out and live on my own. I want somewhere to bring Tara Simmonds-Kendall back to if I ever get her to go out with me.

***

I want to have another look at the rectory, so one Saturday afternoon in the Easter holidays I start up my Fizzy (the only 50cc bike I'm allowed to ride) and tell Mum I'm going to the gym. It's about 3 miles to Southcombe, and I make sure to pack a rucksack full of gym stuff so that she's none the wiser. She's as anal as Dad when it comes to that bloody house, and I've no idea why. I 'liberate' the keys from Dad's desk drawer when he's in the shower.

The rectory gate squeaks as I fling it open, and I decide to push my Fizzy up the drive because I don't like riding on gravel. There's some dude waving to me from the front garden, which is a bit weird, as I had to unlock the gate.

Many questions suddenly buzz around in my head: *Why has he locked himself in? Is he afraid of burglars? Why is he doing gardening if the house is empty? Has Dad kept him on to manage the grounds?* By the amount of weeds and overgrown shrubbery about, I can tell he's not really earning his money.

I walk up to him. He's dressed a bit strangely; the way old men did years ago. I give him a cheesy grin.

"Hi, I'm Ethan."

He's pruning one of the trees by the looks of it. Apart from smiling at me he doesn't come over for a chat. I shrug my shoulders and mutter under my breath.

"Suit yourself."

I take another look at him over my shoulder before I unlock the front door. I must definitely tell the parentals about him. Dad's wasting his money for sure.

There's a damp, musty smell, and it's quite dark inside. I grope around for the light switch, which illuminates the entrance hall. To my surprise a young man and woman come down the stairs, who look a few years older than me. I'm a bit flummoxed to tell the truth, as I thought the house was empty. I keep my voice deliberately unfriendly.

"Hi. Who are you?"

The girl smiles and walks towards me.

"Hello. I'm Mia Finbow." She indicates towards the man. "This is Robbie. We're your half-brother and sister."

You could knock me down with my Fizzy and I'd still not feel it. I stand there, mouth agape, looking at them. The two of them look alike, but they do not resemble me at all. The young man, my half-brother, comes forward and shakes my hand.

"Good morning. I'm Robert Cuthbertson. How d'you do?"

I don't know what's going on. He's dressed similar to how my dad looked in his wedding day photo; long grey tail coat and matching trousers, with a white shirt and grey cravat.

"You getting married, or what?"

My joke is lost on him. My half-sister looks more modern, in designer-torn jeans and fluffy jumper. If she wasn't my sister I'd say she was rather tasty. She laughs and then fixes me with a gimlet eye.

"What are you doing here?"

There's a pregnant pause before I can think of a suitable reply.

"I was going to ask you the same question. It's time I left home, so I was thinking of moving in. But hey, it's a big house. I expect there's room for all of us. Where's your mum then? Does she live here as well?"

I notice the quick glance between them. Mia nods.

"She does, but you wouldn't see her. She knows you're not her son."

These two are doing my head in. I envisage tiptoeing around the house trying not to disturb somebody I'm not supposed to see.

"I'm a brudder from anudder mudder."

Mia giggles, but Robbie appears puzzled. I carry on regardless.

"And who's the dude out in the front garden?"

"Dude?" Robbie looks at me as if I've flown in from Mars. "What's a *dude*?"

"Oh, that's just Max." Mia shrugs. "He does the gardening."

I've no idea why my parents never told me I have a half-brother and sister. There must have been some kind of family war when Dad left their mother and married mine, that's all I can think of. I'm determined to tackle Mum and Dad about it when I get home, but meanwhile these two people I'm related to but don't know at all are in the house that I want to live in. I therefore have to tell them what's on my mind.

"Did Dad give you permission to live here then, or are you squatting?"

Mia chuckles and looks at Robbie, who frowns.

"I'm standing, not squatting." He replies. "We've lived here for years. Our mother was born in this house."

I cannot hide my surprise.

"Really?"

"Yes, really." Robbie shoots me a cold stare. "This is as much my house as yours."

I shrug.

"Well, if you don't mind, then I think I'll join you later in the year."

"Delighted." Robbie's features tell a different story. "There are plenty of spare bedrooms."

CHAPTER 31 - ETHAN

I cane the Fizzy back home as fast as I can, all of 45 miles per hour. I'm angry at being left out in the cold regarding family dynamics. I'm not a kid anymore, and as I ride I think of all the lost years I could have had with my siblings.

Mum's ironing in the dining room as I barge in and slam the door.

"I need to talk to you!"

Mum quietly turns off the iron and stands there facing me.

"If you can talk to me in a reasonable tone, then I'll listen."

I'm almost frothing at the mouth in rage, but I know I'll get nowhere if I start shouting and sounding off on one. Dad appears in the doorway, probably because the walls in this rat-hole are paper thin.

"What's going on?"

I turn around so that I'm looking at both of them.

"I admit I took the keys to the rectory today. I want to live there when I turn eighteen, as you know."

They both look at each other with that knowing glance that in the past has always meant I'm being shut out.

"And?"

Dad's not bollocking me for stealing the keys, so I get into full swing.

"*And….* I only come face to face with Robbie and Mia, who I never knew existed! How could you do that to me? Not to tell a kid he has a brother *and* a sister?"

Mum puts a hand to her mouth in shock, and the colour drains from her face. I've hit a raw nerve here, and I'm determined to milk their treachery to the last drop.

"They said I can move in with them when I'm eighteen, and so I will! Anything's better than living here with you two!"

I push past Dad in the doorway, stomp upstairs to my room and slam the door. I punch the wall to relieve my stress, and my hand shoots right through the thin plasterboard.

"Shit!"

I rub my knuckles and fling myself face down on the bed. Such is my rage that I don't hear Dad come in.

"You've got it all wrong, son."

I turn over and roll my eyes to the ceiling. I can't even bear to look at him.

"I saw them. We chatted. They told me I'm their half-brother."

Dad's voice, when he replies, is eerily calm.

"And so you are, but there's a slight problem."

I prop myself up on one elbow and regard the man I used to idolise.

"So… you admit I've got a brother and sister I never knew existed! What kind of a father are you?"

"One who is trying to protect you." Dad answers. "You see, Ethan … Robbie and Mia are dead. Robbie was stillborn in eighteen sixty eight, and Mia was somehow murdered by her mother Emily a couple of years before you were born. Emily by then had been dead for over a hundred and thirty years, but was as real to me as you are. She obviously wanted both her children with her."

I can't take it in. The man must be on something. Robbie and

Mia were there in front of me as large as life. I've never heard so much *shite*.

"Pull the other one, Dad. It's got bells on. So what you're saying is that you've had a sexual relationship with a ghost?"

"Exactly."

The bloke's as serious as serious can be, but I'm prepared to listen to his ramblings.

"There is only one set of keys, and we keep them here. How do you think they got inside? The gate was locked when you arrived there?"

I nod.

"And did you see a chap working in the garden?"

I feel a bit uneasy, and nod again.

"He worked for Emily's father, the Reverend Cuthbertson, back in the eighteen hundreds. His name was Maxwell Grant. He's buried in Southcombe churchyard, near where Emily is. Ethan, there's no way Mum or I will ever set foot in that house again, and we've never been able to find a buyer for it. I'd rather you didn't go there, but of course once you're eighteen I can't stop you. In the meantime I'm still your guardian, and so I'll have those keys back if you don't mind."

His outstretched hand reaches towards me, and reluctantly I take the keys out of my pocket.

"I suppose you're going to hide them now?"

Dad shakes his head.

"They'll stay in my pocket until you're eighteen, but I hope by then you will see things differently."

***

Dad thinks he knows me, but he doesn't, and I'm determined to prove him wrong. His whole explanation is a lie; I have a brother and sister he doesn't want me to know, probably because he's ashamed of his affair. However, he can't control me when I'm away from the house.

The gym is an excellent excuse to get away, and I'm fairly mobile with the Fizzy. I'm also good at scaling high iron gates, especially the one belonging to Southcombe Rectory.

CHAPTER 32 - ETHAN

I park the Fizzy against the rectory's gate, and scale the top of the ornate ironwork with the aid of extra height gained by climbing on the bike's seat. Within a few moments I'm able to walk up the driveway.

Max stands in the same place in the front garden. It's a bit weird, because that's exactly where he was last time I saw him; he's even pruning the same tree and wearing the same old granddaddy clothes. He waves, and I go up to him.

"Hi Max. I'm Ethan, John Finbow's son."

There's no reply, and he looks away and carries on. However, now I'm up closer I can see he's not making any changes to the tree at all. It's as though he's pruning a *different* one; his fingers work secateurs that fail to cut any branches.

Unsettled, I edge away towards the front door and ring the bell. While I wait for Robbie or Mia to come I take another glance at Max, but I cannot see him anymore.

In my peripheral vision I'm aware of movement at the side of the house. Turning around I see a plump, middle-aged lady.

"Good afternoon. Can I help you?"

She looks the motherly type, but in my wildest nightmares I couldn't imagine my dad ever having sex with her.

"Are you Emily?" I smile as pleasantly as I can. "I'm Ethan, Robbie and Mia's half-brother."

The woman laughs.

"Good heavens, no! I'm Peggy, the housekeeper."

"I've just come to visit my sister and brother. Are they about?"

Peggy beckons me with one hand.

"Come this way. The front door's locked."

***

I follow Peggy along a narrow corridor, but I don't think much cleaning has been done by the look of things. Her and Max must be on a go-slow.

"Wait in the hallway, and they'll be down in a minute."

I watch her bustling off back down the passageway, and then turn around. Robbie and Mia are waiting there at the foot of the stairs. Their sudden arrival seems a little strange because I hadn't heard them come down, and Peggy hadn't called out.

"We meet again." Robert extends his hand in a formal manner. "How are you?"

He's still wearing the same wedding tackle. Mia wears torn jeans and the fluffy jumper she had on before, and her hair is weaved into a long dark plait.

"I'm okay. Did you get married after all?"

He has a sudden puzzled expression. Mia chuckles, and then waves away my remark as she looks at him.

"Don't mind Ethan, he's just joking."

My brother seems as though he's never laughed in his entire life. I try and change the subject.

"I wouldn't mind a drink."

With one hand Robert indicates towards another passageway.

"The kitchen is the last door on the left. Peggy will see to it."

I wander off in the direction he's pointing. Cobwebs hang from the ceiling, and the place is filthy. When I reach the kitchen it's empty, and what's more it doesn't look as though anybody has cooked a meal in it for many years. Grime and dust have settled on every surface. Cupboard doors hang open revealing empty interiors. There is no sign of Peggy, nor any kind of food or drink. I hurry over to the cold tap and turn it on, but only a few drops of rusty water trickle out. Too late I realise why Robert is dressed just like a tailor's dummy.

A cold shiver runs up my back as I realise Dad was right all along; the house hasn't been lived in probably since before I was born. Feeling a little panicky, I make my way back towards the side entrance where I'd first seen Peggy. The door is now locked and there's no sign of a key. I run at top speed in the direction of the main front door, which is shut fast.

I find the front room, where dust sheets cover the few items of furniture left. I throw off one of the sheets, pick up a heavy chair and hurl it at the patio window, which refuses to shatter. Breathing heavily with exertion I stand there and look at Max, who turns around to wave at me from the garden where he's still pruning the same bloody tree.

"You should have listened to your father. This is *my* home. Why have you come here?"

I spin around to find a carbon copy of Mia, although obviously a little older.

I fish around in my pocket for the iPhone I was given at Christmas. Emily looks at it with suspicion as I switch it on.

"What's that?"

"It's a Four G receiver."

"Whatever it is, it'll do you no good here."

She hasn't got a clue that I'll be able to send a text to Dad.

However, as I begin to type a message, the phone leaps out of my hand with a life all its own.

"Somebody needs to teach you some manners."

My heart begins to race with the knowledge that I need to climb to get over the gate and get back to my bike. Something here is very, very wrong.

CHAPTER 33 – JOHN

His dinner sits uneaten on the breakfast bar. Something tells me that Ethan hasn't gone to the gym.

He's a stubborn bugger, just like me. After our recent conversation I've a nasty feeling he might have made a return visit to the rectory. I don't want to alarm Kay, but I can tell she's already anxious.

"Ethan's missed his dinner. It's very unlike him."

I'm not sure how to reply. The slightest inkling that I'm worried as well will set her off on one.

"If you like I'll go to the gym and see if I can find him."

She runs off to get her coat, so I've no doubt she intends to come with me. However, she's unwittingly saved from a fate worse than death by an impromptu visit from Lana. I slip out quietly while they're chatting; there's no way I'll ever let her step inside that house again.

I by-pass the gym and head straight for the rectory. I'm correct in my assumption; Ethan's bike is right outside. My heart sinks into my boots as I park the car next to his bike and then unlock the gate. Fortunately it's too dark to see whether Mad Max is outside waving his shears, and to be honest I'd rather not know.

The house is in darkness, and that worries me greatly. I unlock the front door quietly, and grope along the wall for the light switch.

Fortunately Steve finished all the work he was paid for, but funnily enough I never heard from him again.

She's already standing in the hallway. I swallow down the lump at the back of my throat.

"Hello Emily. I've come to get Ethan and then we'll leave you in peace."

She regards me with a kind of haughty and aloof air.

"John, nice of you to drop by after eighteen years."

I back up with one fist on the open door handle.

"You got what *you* wanted. Now I'm here to get what *I* want."

The icy blue eyes shoot through me like arrows.

"Don't you think it would be a nice idea for a father to meet his two other children after all this time? We're a *family*, and you haven't been near nor by."

All I want to do is grab Ethan and run, but it seems that isn't going to be possible. Very reluctantly I let go of the door handle.

"Sure. Just as long as Ethan's here with them."

"Wait here." She nods and turns around to face the stairs. "I'll bring them down."

My heart's hammering like it wants to jump out of my chest as I stand there figuring how long it'll take Ethan and me to leg it back to the car. Presently there's movement on the mezzanine floor above, and the four of them come out of Emily's bedroom. Ethan looks the same as he always does, but there's something wrong with his eyes; they're not Ethan's eyes. He doesn't wave or acknowledge me at all.

"Look at your lovely children, John." Emily makes a sweeping wave in their direction. "Yours and ours. How they love their father."

Nobody's smiling much. It's all a bit surreal. I hold out my hand in Ethan's direction.

"Come on, son. Let's go home to Mum."

He doesn't move. Emily chuckles.

"He *is* home. He's the anchor that will keep you here with your rightful family."

The penny drops.

I start to run; first the kitchen down the hallway, which is empty and dark. Next the dining room – similarly bereft of life and hope. I crash into the front room and switch on the light. There he lies next to an upturned chair, his iPhone buzzing next to him with message after message from Kay.

He's a big lad, but I've suddenly been blessed with a strength I didn't know I had. He's bleeding from one wrist, and blood is seeping into the filthy, faded carpet. I put his phone in his pocket, pick him up bodily, and run towards the front door.

"He has no life left in him!" Emily tries unsuccessfully to block my path. "You are wasting your time!"

His eyelids flicker, which tells me a different story.

***

I don't care if I break the speed limit. I hit 72 miles an hour in a 30 zone and Brackenrye Hospital's A&E entrance approaches within a short time. Ethan's unconscious now, and time is of the essence. I leave the car where it is right outside the door; to hell with parking clamps. I pick him up from the front seat as though he was still two years old, and run like I've never done before; legs, arms and chest straining with the effort.

"Please help my son!" I gasp at the receptionist. "He's lost a lot of blood! He's type O positive!"

The staff immediately take over and Ethan's wheeled into a cubicle straight away. His breathing is very shallow. I sink down into a chair next to him while his wound is dressed and the medics expertly hook him up to a transfusion drip, which to my relief soon begins a steady journey through his veins. My limbs feel leaden, and

I realise I haven't even phoned Kay.

As though on cue, the iphone buzzes in my pocket. I don't even feel as though I have the strength to pick it up, but pick it up I must. Kay's face smiles up at me from the display screen. I hate myself for having let her down. I've been such a total and utter arsehole. If it takes me forever to make it up to her, then so be it.

"Hello love." I sigh. "Ethan's in A and E. I'll explain when you get here."

There's nothing more I can do for my son except hold his hand. I stand up and grab his fingers, which feel somewhat clammy.

"Dad's here. I love you, son." My eyes fill up, but I carry on. "You're going to be alright, and Mum's on her way. Squeeze my hand if you can hear me."

There's a very faint tremble of his fingers. I let the tears fall and give thanks to a God that for most of my adult life I haven't needed to speak to. I hope He can still hear me.

CHAPTER 34 – JOHN

While Ethan recovers at home I hatch a plan in my head that will finally rid us of Emily, and for once in my life I'm glad I live on a council estate.

Every Friday night we have Ethan's favourite meal. No gourmet concoctions for him, just plain old fish and chips from the chippy down the road. I leave him palely loitering on the settee with his mother keeping her devoted watch, and wearing my most deadbeat attire slink off towards where the usual hooded youth stands freezing his nuts off on the junction of Ferris Street and Crozier Road. The youth regards me with some surprise.

"Want some skunk?"

I shake my head.

"You and your mates want to earn some real money?"

There's suspicion on his features, but I can also tell that cash registers are already ringing up possible rewards in what passes for his brain.

"Yeah. What have I got to do?"

"Meet me here with three of your mates at nine o'clock tomorrow night. Wear gloves. Five thousand quid each before the job, and five thousand each afterwards. But this goes no further ... right? If it does, I'll be round to the pigs straight away and let them know about your little drug-dealing empire."

I whip out my phone and take a quick photo as he stands there open-mouthed.

"I'll give them your mugshot as well."

"Fuck!" The youth tries to grab my phone. "No pictures!"

I stash the phone in the inside pocket of my jacket, and give him my most beatific smile.

"'Course not – it's just for insurance."

***

There they are; four deadbeat gloved and hooded teenagers who wait impatiently at the junction as I stroll nonchalantly towards them.

"Evening boys."

The one blessed with a speck of grey matter manages a few grunts.

"Where we goin' then?"

"That's for me to know." I waggle a finger at him. "When we get there I'll give you five thousand each for starters."

There's a whisper of approval amongst the ranks. Four toe-rags, one twice the size of the other three, follow me like ducklings when I turn around and begin to walk towards the car.

"Three of you in the back and one in the front. I don't care who sits where."

Not a word is spoken as we head off towards Southcombe, and I park the car a little bit away from the rectory down a quiet lovers' lane. The Neanderthals crowd around me as I dish out bulging envelopes of money under the cover of darkness like Lord Bountiful. After checking that my word is as good as my bond, they stash their loot about their unattractive persons. I give them a thumbs up.

"Look after it, lads. There's more after the job's done." I unlock the boot of the car. "Now make yourselves useful, and grab a rucksack each. They're heavy 'cause there's a can of petrol inside."

Knowing looks ricochet around between them. I dish out a box of matches to each youth, then point them in the direction of the rectory and start walking.

"I'll unlock the gate and the front door. Don't worry – nobody's at home. I should know, because I own it. Just burn the fucking place down to the ground and then leg it back to the car. There's another five thousand each in my inside jacket pocket when the place is alight. I'll go for a little walk when I've opened the door, and then I'll leave you to it. I'll be looking out for the flames, and the car will stay unlocked for when you're done. Bring back the rucksacks and petrol cans, and put them in the boot."

Grey Matter's face is wreathed in smiles.

"Say no more." He holds up a box of matches. "Enjoy your walk."

***

Church Lane is deserted as I stroll along, checking for any signs of life. As soon as I reach the gates and look down the driveway I can see orange flames of fire licking at some of the windows. I run back to the car to where all four boys, breathless and sweaty, have flung themselves.

"I'll just lock up again and then I'll be back."

My hands, enclosed in gloves, are hot. I fumble with the keys, managing to lock the front door as a blaze crackles and roars in the hallway. Somewhere to the back of the house there is a small explosion. I run to the gate, lock it, and sprint back to the car in record time. Maybe Max was waving goodbye, but I didn't dare look. There's a smell of petrol and soot when I open the car door.

"Cheers lads. I'll drive for a bit and then you can have the rest of the money."

It's a relief to get away from the house. I hope that nobody spots the fire until every room is a heap of cinders.

CHAPTER 35 – ETHAN

Something's going on, but I'm not sure what. The police have arrived and there's murmuring in the front room. Dad had previously told me he'd driven at 72 miles an hour to get me to A&E, so perhaps it's about that.

I decide to saunter downstairs and see what I can find out. It's probably gone viral that a police car has pulled up outside. Okay so it's not an unusual sight on this estate, but it is outside our place.

As if on cue, the phone buzzes in my pocket with an incoming call. I have a quick look at the screen, rush back upstairs, and accept the call from my cousin Barry. I don't even let him speak.

"It's none of your fucking business."

I can hear him roaring with laughter at the other end.

"Go on, spill the beans. Have you been dealing crack down at the chippy?"

"Yeah." I hiss. "*And* outside the school gates."

Barry is not to be deterred.

"Come on, out with it."

I sigh.

"I've no more of an idea than you have. The police are in the front room with Mum and Dad. I was just going downstairs to find out, but then some dick phoned."

He's alright, is Baz; a bit cocky, but then you have to be around here otherwise you'd go under.

"Let me know, yeah?"

I end the call just as the front room door opens. Two cops emerge; one of them is a woman who looks rather tasty in her uniform. As soon as they leave I look at Dad questioningly.

"What's going on?"

Mum and Dad look a bit grim, and I wonder if someone's died. Dad looks at Mum before speaking.

"It's the rectory. It's been burned to the ground."

I'm absolutely gobsmacked. I'd changed my mind about living there of course, but never thought something like this would ever happen.

"What!" I shout in reply. "Who would have done that?"

Dad shrugs.

"That's what the police want to find out."

I grab the Fizzy's keys from a side table.

"I'm going to have a look."

Mum stands in my way. I'm at least a foot taller than her, but the red hair ensures she can be rather fierce if she wants to be.

"You will do no such thing! Look what happened the last time you went there!"

I put on my best pacifying tone.

"Dad's just said the house has gone, Mum. What danger could there be? I'll only go up to the main gate."

"We'll both go." Dad butts in. "I want to see if there's anything left."

***

Several fire engines are still parked up on the driveway when we arrive, to the dismal sight of a smouldering ruin in front of us.

Blackened, twisted girders and rubble lie scattered about, and there's an acrid sooty smell in the air. One side wall is still standing, joined onto a stub of the back wall leading out to where the patio used to be. A fireman spots us and hurries over.

"It's too dangerous to come any nearer."

Dad clears his throat.

"I'm the owner. Any idea what started it?"

"Not yet." The fireman shakes his head. "We'll be investigating, along with the police."

"Dodgy wiring?" I venture timidly.

Dad shrugs.

"Who knows? We may never find out."

The fireman looks surprised.

"If it's arson, we can usually discover the accelerant by using sniffer dogs, pouring patterns, and even by gas chromatography and mass spectrometry of debris samples in the lab. There's often a way to find out if a fire has been caused deliberately, or if it's just an accident."

Dad doesn't answer. We look around at the devastation in what used to be the front garden. It's a sad ending for such a beautiful old house.

***

Dad's still not saying anything as he starts the car up. I decide to break the silence.

"What will you do about the rubble?"

Dad shifts into first gear and moves slowly along Church Lane. There's a group of rubberneckers standing near the gates. I feel like sticking my middle finger up at them.

"Get a demolition team in to clear the site when the fire bods have finished with it, and then I'll sell the land probably. Some developer will rub his hands together and want to build fifty flats on it."

"Why don't you keep the land?" I turn to look at him. "You could build another large house on it and rent it out."

"Nah." He replies quite emphatically. "I just want to get rid of it."

CHAPTER 36 – JOHN

Okay, so the lab guys have found out the fire was caused by petrol, but I'm sure we'll get away with it just as long as the four deadheads keep quiet. What's the point of them speaking out? They'll only incriminate themselves.

The Press are having a field day with the first bit of local news in months. I really didn't want to be on the front page of the Southcombe Standard, but it would have looked suspicious if I'd refused. The Neanderthals probably can't even read, and so with a bit of luck they won't realise I live just a few streets away from them.

When the hubbub dies down a bit, the demolition team and land clearance guys move in. I'm so glad to see flat, even ground when they're finished that I want to do a little dance. Nothing is left; only the boundary walls and two iron gates.

To my great surprise, nobody comes forward to buy the land. After advertising extensively without success, Ethan's idea of building another house on the site begins to gnaw away at my brain. Kay puts in her two pence worth.

"It'll be an investment for our old age if you get writer's block. You can't just waste all that land. *I* don't want to live there, but you never know…*somebody* might."

I shrug.

"I'll think about it."

I've already thought about it. It's all systems go as far as I'm concerned.

***

I get a call from the police; they've arrested one of the deadheads, Kelvin Smith, who has been splashing his money around. He's let off without charge, but as sure as eggs is eggs I know what's coming next. Sure enough, there's a knock at my door one evening a few months after the fire. There he stands. Kelvin, the pimply youth with bags full of skunk.

"I asked around a bit."

"So?" I shrug, ignore my hammering heart, and give him my best disinterested yawn.

"*So…* we want more money."

I hear Kay coming down the hallway, and step out into the garden.

"Listen, you little shithead." I close the door behind me. "I've still got that photo, remember? It's on my hard drive, so why don't you just piss off and relay the bad news to your pals?"

He stabs me with an imaginary dagger before slinking off into the abyss from whence he came, but Kay's already opened the door.

"Who was that?"

"Oh, just someone looking for Ethan. When he gets home I'll let him know."

I must have sounded convincing, because the first thing she did when Ethan arrived back from his girlfriend's house was to blurt out how some skinny youth in a hoody had come calling for him, causing our son to appear unsurprisingly clueless.

"Don't worry." I quickly interjected. "He probably had the wrong house."

I want to get the hell out of this bloody sink estate. Enough is enough.

***

I have this vision of the perfect house in my mind; swimming pool in the basement, then upstairs to two huge ground floor reception rooms, separate dining room, fabulous kitchen with every type of modern convenience to keep Kay happy, utility room for all the white goods, and a cloakroom/bathroom and study. Up on the first floor would be at least 5 bedrooms with en-suite bathrooms and walk-in wardrobes, one huge his and hers bathroom, and a separate shower room. Every room would have push-button controls to open or close the curtains, activate any hi-fi system and TV, and to control the air temperature.

I put it to Kay, and she drools over the fabulous kitchen bit, air-conditioning, his and hers bathroom, and walk-in wardrobes. Ethan seems up for the idea, but has all his friends in Broadberry and so does not want to move too far away. Five acres of land that I already own stands cleared and ready for architect's plans three miles away in Southcombe.

I snuggle up to Kay in bed and give her a squeeze.

"We have enough money to build the house of our dreams. The land is all cleared at Southcombe. We could start all over again."

There is a deathly silence for several agonising minutes before she pipes up.

"What about the un-lovely Emily?"

I keep my voice light and unconcerned.

"The demolition guys never mentioned anything untoward. Every time I've been over there I've seen nothing. The fire wiped them all out, I think."

"I don't know." Kay sighs. "I don't want to go through all that again."

I prop myself up on one elbow and look down at her.

"Come over with me and see the ground." I kiss the top of her head. "There's nothing left for them to haunt."

"She completely took you over." Kay stares at me. "You realise that, don't you? And look what she did to *me!*"

"Yes." I nod. "I'm so sorry. You know I had no control over it."

"Yes, I figured that one out." Kay replies. "And that's what makes her so dangerous."

"Just come with me tomorrow." I cuddle back down beside her. "You'll see what I mean.

***

I open the iron gates and the three of us stand there for some time without speaking. Eventually Ethan walks forward, holds his arms out and runs, pseudo-flying around the inside of the boundary walls. I feel like humming the Dam Busters' tune.

"Look at all this space, Dad!" Ethan shouts at us as he runs. "We'll have the best house in the area!"

Kay takes tentative steps inside the grounds and smiles at our son's antics.

"I'd be happier if Coral comes here just to make sure."

"Of course." I'd agree to anything she asks just to get off the estate. "Ring her up as soon as you like."

"I'll do that." She replies. "If Coral says it's okay, then call the architects in. And my sisters can stay?"

I plant a smackeroo on her cheek.

"Any time they like."

I'm so happy. I waltz Kay around the rubble as Ethan runs out of aviation fuel and comes to a halt.

"What the hell are you two doing?"

"We're dancing." I laugh. "Dancing for joy."

CHAPTER 37 – KAY

Coral's moved away, and I don't have her new address or phone number. I Google local mediums, but none of them get back to me. I must have some sort of confirmation that Emily and the rest of them have shuffled off to the celestial fields. John's impatient to call the architects in and get his new project going, so I look a bit further afield and find a London medium willing to travel to Southcombe. I arrange to meet with Suzann Walters at the old rectory site. She has glowing reviews on her website, and although her charges are high I find this somehow reassuring.

Suzann steps smiling out of what looks like a brand new Audi a week later. She's younger than I thought, and I notice the designer clothes and handbag. As I unlock the gates I turn and speak to her over my shoulder.

"Thanks for making the trip up here."

"No problem at all." Suzann replies. "I was intrigued at your story."

She walks along what used to be the gravel drive. Some of the gravel is still intact, and her stilettos are perhaps not one of her better ideas.

"I see a huge Victorian house in my mind's eye."

"That's right." I nod. "It had eight bedrooms."

"One family lived here happily for many years."

John would say that she'd probably done meticulous research on Google, but she's pleasant, and I want to give her the benefit of the doubt.

"Do you see anybody in particular, Suzann?"

I look around the remains. The site is empty, and somehow bleak.

"I sense an elderly man dressed in black. He wears a clerical collar."

I'm surprised that Reverend Cuthbertson has made an appearance. John had never mentioned seeing him before.

"Anybody else?" I venture hopefully. "Do you sense any evil presence?"

"No." Suzann shakes her head. "Nobody else at all."

I lock up, part with £80 and drive away, puzzled. I mention Suzann's findings to John and Ethan at dinner.

"She only sensed a man in a clerical collar and nobody else, and so I assume it was Emily's father?"

John nods.

"Yes, sounds like it. That's good news then."

Ethan shovels half a roll into his mouth. I wish he wouldn't do that.

"When can the architect get going, Dad?"

"As soon as Mum's happy."

They both look at me for an answer. I can't say I'm absolutely convinced that Emily isn't there, but then again I don't want to be a party pooper.

"Okay." I hold up my hands in supplication. "Do your worst."

John's on the phone almost straight away. However, it'll be interesting to discover whether the architects or builders report any paranormal activity.

***

I change my shopping preference to the supermarket in Southcombe. In this way I can pass by the building site every week and watch our house take shape. The diggers move in soon after the plans are drawn up, and begin to carve out what will be our swimming pool. I must say, it *is* rather exciting, and I feel guilty that I've made John stay for so long on the estate against his will.

The police seem no nearer to finding out who set the rectory alight. My theory is that it was just bored teenagers mucking about in an old, disused house, and their game got out of hand. Whoever it was, John doesn't seem too bothered about it.

It's only when I forget some milk and pootle down to the 7/11 on the estate that my theory falls flat. On exiting the shop, there's a thin, pimply youth sitting on a concrete block opposite; I think I've seen him about before. As I walk back home I become aware of a presence some distance behind me. Instinct kicks in. I grab my phone and turn it on to video, walking more quickly while keeping the phone hidden in my pocket. When I turn around I feel slightly panicky that he's only a matter of inches away from me.

"Lady, you need to tell your old man something from me."

I swallow hard, feign indifference, and slide the phone out of my pocket.

"And who might you be?"

"Never mind who I am." The youth waves my question away. "He needs to pay me ten thousand like I told him, or we'll burn down your new house as well. Yeah, I read about that in the *Standard*."

I let my left arm hang down, but slant the phone upwards in my hand. The fifty pound notes in his eyes have blinded him.

"You burned down the rectory?"

"Yeah." The youth grins menacingly. "And we'll do it again if he doesn't pay."

I think I've filmed enough evidence. I slide the phone back.

"I'll have a word with my husband."

"You do that."

The youth's halitosis makes me want to retch. I swallow again and move backwards.

"I'll get him to go to the bank first thing tomorrow when it opens."

I can't wait to get home.

***

The TV is on when I arrive home. I quickly lock the door behind me, and then lean momentarily against the door's wooden panel, pleased to have returned home in one piece. John comes out into the hallway.

"You okay?"

"Yes." I sigh. "Some yob followed me home and says he'll burn down our new house unless you pay him ten thousand pounds. I got him on my phone though."

John's genial expression changes to worried in an instant. All at once he's on edge and distant.

"Let me see."

"Did you know who set light to the rectory then?" I pass him the phone. "Why didn't you go to the police?"

"I'm not sure he *did* do it. I think he's just after money."

"So he's spoken to you too?" I reply. "Why didn't you say something?"

John doesn't answer, and just stares at the short video. Presently he laughs.

"Good! That's enough evidence to go to the police with! You've got his face! That's Kelvin Smith!" He kisses me smack on the mouth. "Well done!"

I was only running on instinct, but am glad I've been of some use. Just because we've got money, it seems that everybody wants some of it, especially on this estate, which has definitely gone downhill in the past few years. Perhaps it'll be better if we live behind locked gates after all. I look at John questioningly.

"Can we increase the security at the new place? Change the gates and install a webcam?"

He nods in agreement.

"Of course. That's just what I was thinking."

I cannot wait to move.

CHAPTER 38 – JOHN

The police re-arrest and charge Kelvin Smith on the evidence filmed by Kay. Of course he incriminates me, as for once he's telling the truth. However, due to his past drug-dealing record, the police have no trouble believing me when, outraged, I protest my total innocence.

The judge sends him down for two years, as everyone knows the house was empty in the first place. To ensure a shorter sentence of just 18 months, the bastard grasses up Jayden Laming, Tyler Brown, and another arsehole, Wayne Webster, much to their discontent, and all four will thankfully soon be residing at Her Majesty's pleasure. I hear on the local grapevine muttered threats of death and destruction aimed at us when they've served their sentences, but keep the unwelcome news from Kay and Ethan.

The underclass of Broadberry estate are not much in my mind during meetings with the architects and commencement of construction at the old rectory site. It's very exciting seeing the house of our dreams taking shape, and I find myself driving down there most days to oversee the work. Two JCB diggers have excavated a swimming-pool sized hole in no time at all. The builders do not report any untoward sightings, and I start to relax and assume the fire burned away any wandering Victorian spirits. I even visit Emily's grave, but walk away unaffected.

I can't settle to writing. As the years have rolled by, my enthusiasm has waned somewhat. We have enough money to live on for the rest of our lives, and for the moment all I want to do is move away from the hell on earth that is the Broadberry Estate.

I'm antsy, and start clearing out the loft in preparation for the eventual shift back to Southcombe. I thought we'd removed all Mia's clothes and toys years ago, but Kay must have saved some as keepsakes. I come across a suitcase crammed with my daughter's little baby suits, cardigans and dresses, and even her favourite scrap of blanket that she wouldn't go to sleep without. I haven't cried for God knows how long, but in the privacy of the loft I let a river of tears fall into that suitcase. However, a sensible, nagging voice in my head tells me it's time to burn the lot and move on.

***

By the late summer of 2018 the house is coming along nicely. The walls, floorboards and staircases are up, the roof is on, and the three of us take much delight in walking through the unfinished rooms after the builders leave for the day. Okay, it's dangerous on a building site and visiting after hours is forbidden, but we, the new owners, have the keys to the new security gate and mean no harm.

One evening Ethan stands at an open hole in one of the walls and looks down onto what will be the back patio, while a warm breeze lifts a fringe of auburn hair on his forehead.

"This is *my* room."

I walk up to stand beside him, and put an arm casually around his shoulders.

"Yeah." I laugh. "This is *your* room."

He sighs.

"When will it all be done, Dad?"

I sense his impatience, as I too am suffering from the same condition.

"Probably another year yet. The electricians, glaziers, plumbers, plasterers, interior designers and swimming pool teams have to come in. Then the grounds have to be landscaped as well.

I turn eastwards towards the boundary wall at a sudden movement.

"Oh Christ! I don't believe it!"

Ethan follows my direction, and I hear him take an inward breath.

Over near the wall, Maxwell Grant prunes a long dead tree that only he can see. It's like fucking Groundhog Day. The two of us stand there transfixed at the sight of him. When he finishes his task, he turns around to us and gives us a hearty wave just as Kay runs upstairs, breathless.

"They've even built three changing rooms near the pool!"

I pull my arm down and elbow Ethan gently in the ribs, who is wonderfully quick on the uptake.

"Hey, that's great!" I reply in hopefully an upbeat voice.

Kay comes over to what will be the window of Ethan's room.

"What are you two looking at?"

"Oh … nothing." I tear my gaze away from Max. "We're just trying to imagine how the grounds will look."

"I want a summerhouse over *there*." She points to beyond where the patio will be. "I can sit in there with my book."

How can I let her down now, after all she's gone through? The walls are the same, but the house is different and what's more it's over half completed and paid for. I fervently hope it's just Max who has returned to his old haunting ground.

***

Back at home I pop in to say goodnight to Ethan. He's asleep with headphones on. I gently remove them and his iPlayer, and he stirs before opening his eyes.

"I thought Mum paid for a medium?"

I sit down on the end of his bed.

"Yeah, but some bloody medium she turned out to be."

He asks the question I knew would be coming.

"Do you still want to move there, Dad?"

I nod.

"Mum can't wait, and we've only seen Max don't forget."

Ethan props himself up and yawns.

"Charlie from school wants to backpack around France fruit-picking and doing bar work for a few months now we're on our gap year. He's asked me to go with him. Can we stay at the house at Saint Tropez if and when we get there?"

Our son is 18 now and a young man. What can I do but wish him well?

"Of course." I smile at him, already feeling pangs of separation, mostly in my wallet. "Enjoy your freedom before Uni."

CHAPTER 39 – KAY

My baby has gone off to do God knows what with his rucksack and his best friend – all 6 foot 2 inches of him. I didn't really want Ethan to go, but what can I do? The boy is supposedly an adult. He says he'll be back at Christmas and will find himself a job until Uni begins. He also has a set of keys to our summer house in Saint Tropez; I just hope he doesn't turn it into a temporary brothel.

The house is unusually quiet, and John seems rather subdued. I expect he's missing Ethan just as much as I am, although I am glad our son is away from the undesirables on the estate. Everywhere you go there seems to be tattooed youths standing on corners looking shifty. Some of them even spit at me when I go down to the supermarket, and I'm getting scared to venture out now. I've no idea why they hate me so much. It can't be anything to do with the fire, so perhaps they know we've got money and are jealous. I'm glad my nephews and nieces live so near, and it feels good to know I have a supportive family. I think from what Katy says, her boys, Thomas and Billy, have warned the yobs from coming too near our front door.

John doesn't go over to the new house so much now. The novelty's worn off, and he's trying to write another screenplay. The builders keep him updated though, and from what I can gather the windows have been fitted and the plasterers will soon be doing their magic with the walls after the electricians have bashed out channels for wires and installed the fire and burglar alarm systems.

It's October – the season of mellow fruitfulness, or is that September? Whatever it is, it's two months until Ethan returns home. I need to keep busy, and so I think I'll call Percy Ye Myint back, and we can go over some fabrics and designs for curtains and carpets. John doesn't care what colour scheme the rooms have, just as long as he gets to decorate his own study. It's like moving into the rectory all over again, but this time without Emily.

***

I've started to order food online now. I really dislike going to the supermarket on the estate, as I'm aware I stop the conversation every time I walk in there. I know I can drive a bit further afield to Southcombe, and have a few times, but it's actually easier now to have it all delivered. John and I are actively disliked now, our car was splashed with paint overnight last week, and I can sense everyone's eyes on me if I venture out the door. John is quiet too, and I am determined to tackle him about it.

I serve his favourite meal; fillet steak, chips, mushrooms, boiled tomatoes and peas, and wait until he's swallowed the last mouthful.

"That was lovely, Kay." John wipes his mouth and smiles at me. "The steak was cooked just right."

"Glad you liked it." I put down my knife and fork. "John…"

He looks at me with interest.

"What?"

"Is there something wrong? You've been very quiet lately. Is it because the yobs are getting to you?"

He shrugs.

"I was upset about the paint, but hey, we'll be moving in short while. We'll just have to live with it, unless we put our stuff in storage and stay in a hotel. Ethan's not back until Christmas. We can do that if you like."

"No, let's not spend money unnecessarily." I shake my head. "Ethan needs a home to come back to. We'll stick it out. It's only for a few more months."

He was upset *before* the paint strike, so if anything is bothering him I realise straight away that I'll have to try and dig a bit deeper.

After we've loaded the dishwasher I cuddle up to him on the sofa and press the remote to activate the TV.

"What do you want to watch tonight?"

Once again he seems distant, and the reply takes longer than usual to arrive.

"Oh…I don't care. Anything you like."

I flick through the channels, but then am startled by the sound of breaking glass. Both of us jump up terrified as a brick hurtles through our window and lands with a thud on the carpet at our feet.

"Christ!" John yells. "Run and stay in the kitchen!"

All at once he's hurrying to the front door. I pick up the brick, which has a message attached to it with a length of string, and run towards the back of the house. I hear John opening our front door and shouting obscenities into the night. I've read the note by the time he comes in.

"The bastards have run away. There's nobody there now."

He's angrier than I've seen him in a long time. I hold out the note.

"John, what does this mean? It says that *you* started the fire and it should be *you* who's inside, not the people you paid to do your dirty work."

He takes the note from me. I can see his hands are shaking.

"They're making stuff up." He replies and flops down onto a chair at the kitchen table. "Perhaps it *is* time to get out of here."

We have lived on the estate for many years, and have not previously caused the wrath of our local criminal fraternity. Something has happened. Nobody gets a brick through their window for no reason. I look at my husband.

"You organised for the rectory to be burned down, didn't you?"

To my horror, he sighs and slumps forward with elbows on the table.

"Yeah. I wanted it and Emily gone. Now it's done. Forget about it and look forward to moving into your new home."

I cannot believe my ears. My husband has just admitted he was behind the fire that four young men are serving prison sentences for. I move my head slowly from side to side.

"John… what the hell have you done? No wonder I can't walk down the street to the supermarket anymore! What's next? Petrol through the letterbox when we're asleep?"

"I'll sort it." He replies. "I don't know how yet, but I'll sort it."

CHAPTER 40 – JOHN

There's no way I'm going to the police. Therefore I realise there's only one thing for it; I visit the bastards in prison and ask for an address so that I can send cheques to their families through the post. The looks on their faces are a picture when I walk in, but I have an idea the bricks and threats will soon be a thing of the past when their relatives open the envelopes.

Kay thinks I'm a stupid fucker for contacting the yobs in the first place. She's not talking much at the moment, and that makes two of us. After spotting Max I'm still worried the fire hasn't got rid of Emily, but we'll only find that out with time. I only ever saw Max in the garden, and the ground by the wall where he stands wasn't affected. I'm certain she's gone; the builders would have said something if she's still there, I'm sure.

I think Kay misses Ethan. I do too, and talking on Skype isn't quite the same. I can see he's arrived at Saint Tropez with his pal, and is probably doing all the things I did at 18, judging by the two attractive girls sitting on my settee. The boy has gone and a young man, a bit more worldly-wise, will be returning to us at Christmas I expect.

***

And so he does, although he goes out a lot of the time. He's still got a bit of a tan, and his biceps are more developed. I'm turning into an old man, and he's suddenly getting a lot of interest from girls on the estate. The phone rings as soon as he's home, and girls come to the door and leave notes through the letterbox instead of petrol. I think he's found out what his todger is for, and I just hope no irate father presses the doorbell with a shotgun in his hand. I suppose I'll have to give him one of those embarrassing-for-both-of-us man to man chats at some point.

The chance comes as we check out the new wiring after electricians have given us welcome illumination in the house. There's no sign of Max in the garden, and we go round the rooms giggling and flicking switches on and off like naughty schoolboys. Ethan looks approvingly around his bedroom

"Won't be long until I can get my new bed! Mum says I can have a double."

I clear my throat.

"Got someone in mind for the other half?"

He taps his nose and doesn't even blush.

"Might have."

"Er…" I inwardly cringe before continuing. "I hope you're using johnny's."

"Johnny's *what*?" He laughs. "Don't worry, Dad. Mum's already given me the lecture. Anyway, girls are always on the pill."

I hide my relief.

"They might not be, son. If they want to get away from their parents, the council will give them a house if they've got a kid. Be wary."

I catch a quick look of surprise on his face before it's gone forever. *Ah well, at least he knows now.*

***

For Christmas day we're treated to the delights of Denise. Denise is a rather shapely girl who makes constant cow eyes at Ethan across the table. I feel like Methuselah's grandfather, but Kay's taking it all in her stride. I carve the turkey and pass a plateful to Ethan, who now seems to be eating us out of house and home all the time.

I want him to learn the value of money, and not take it for granted. He's stuffing his face with money I've earned through my own efforts, and I suddenly think back to how hard life was for me at his age.

"Have you been job-hunting since you've been back from France?"

Denise turns her limpid brown pools onto Ethan and waits, as I do, for an answer to my question.

"I don't need to. Denise's Dad says I can work with him in his scrapyard."

Good old Denise's Dad, whoever he may be.

"That's great." I pass a plate of turkey towards Denise. "Give your dad my regards."

"Will do." She giggles. "He can start on the seventh of January and work there until we go to Australia."

"Australia?" Kay chips in, fork halted a few inches from her lips.

"Yeah." Ethan nods. "We want to see Australia in the spring. Won't get another chance once Uni starts."

I can't help a niggling annoyance building up.

"And who's paying for this little jaunt?"

"*I am*, Dad." My son looks me straight in the eyes. "I've money saved up from working in France, and I'll earn more in the scrapyard and from working when I get out there. You don't need to pay me a penny."

I nearly choke on my turkey. Our son is growing up to be quite a remarkable young man.

"Great!" I reply with genuine warmth. "You can have the air fare. In fact I'll pay for both of you."

CHAPTER 41 – KAY

It's getting exciting now. I've finalised the interior designs with Percy, and when all the floor coverings are in place then we can have lots of lovely furniture delivered. We decided to start all over again with new sofas, armchairs, beds, wardrobes, desks, and kitchen and bathroom equipment, and so we're not taking much from this house. I've told Ethan he can sell most of it to fund his trip to Australia. He leaves in a month's time, but we'll be in the new house by then. We decided to call it Southcombe Hall; I think it sounds quite grand. We sold our present home back to the council for a ridiculously cheap price just to get rid of it quickly. The council are desperate to house asylum seekers, and jumped at the chance.

I heard on the grapevine that the four Neanderthals will be let out early on good behaviour. This is even more of a reason for us to leave the estate. Everything we're taking is more or less in boxes now, and I can't wait to unpack and get everything straight. My sense of order has all gone to pot, as nothing is where it ought to be.

I tag along with John one evening about a week before we move, when he announces that he's driving over to the Hall to check the recently installed fire alarm system. I've started riding pillion now on the back of his bike. It's only a few miles there, and it's a great feeling zipping along in and out of the traffic. John's a very competent driver, and there's a weird sense of freedom as the wind blows down the front of your neck that you don't get inside a car. When he 'gives it a handful' I get a little tingle of fear at the bike's latent power, but somehow feel strangely young again.

He stops the Harley on our new tarmacked drive, and I dismount first.

"Better than gravel for the bike, eh?" I take off my crash helmet and leave it on the seat. "Not so slippery?"

"Yeah." John stares hard at the boundary wall. "Less chance of going arse over tit."

I follow his gaze to where our newly-laid lawn meets the wall. The original brickwork is now crumbling in places.

"Time to get it re-built?"

"That's a good idea." He nods in agreement. "I've got a brickie friend who'd love to give us a quote. Pity I didn't think of that before. Then none of it will be Victorian."

We walk up to the main door, built of solid oak and hopefully able to withstand a siege. Once inside, John looks approvingly around the entrance hall.

"The sparkys have put sprinklers in every room that run off the mains water, and the alarm system auto-dials via the telephone line straight to the fire brigade in case the electric goes out. They've put loads of extinguishers everywhere."

He trots over to where a panel of buttons and an intercom has been installed at the foot of the stairs, and points towards a large red indicator button currently glowing 'on'.

"We can turn it on and off here, by pressing that red button. The black button below opens the front gate, and whoever's there can speak to us here in the house."

It all looks easy enough, and I feel comforted by its presence. I give a hollow laugh.

"Shame the rectory didn't have this."

He doesn't answer.

***

We only take one lorry-load of goods and chattels with us on the actual day of moving. Ethan has sold most of our furniture to University students looking to upgrade their rooms, and it's a happy threesome who cross the threshold of Southcombe Hall at the beginning of March 2019. John carries me over as though we're newlyweds, while Ethan races up to his room to get away from his embarrassing parents.

"Put me down!" I protest weakly "I want to start unpacking!"

There's a faint old man noise as John lowers me to the ground.

"Good job I've got my truss on."

I smack his behind, and sigh with happiness. The house is huge, compared to where we've come from. As I remember it's even bigger than the original rectory.

"Is the pool ready to swim in?"

John nods.

"Ready to rock. Are you going skinny dipping then?"

"Not when Ethan's about." I laugh in reply.

The removal men brush past us with the first of the boxes.

"Shame." John gives me a wink. "Still, it'll give me something to look forward to."

He goes off to give them a hand, and I wander into the kitchen to unpack the first box. It's full of our old crockery and plates, but I rapidly come to the conclusion that this house needs the finest bone china. I make a mental note to take a trip to Knightsbridge in the near future.

CHAPTER 42 – JOHN

The new house is everything I've ever dreamed of. It's spacious and roomy, but feels homely at the same time. I approve of Percy's interior designs, and have even allowed him into my study to do his thing.

With Ethan gone off to the other side of the world, Kay and I christened the pool in our birthday suits last night. This led of course to what you'd normally imagine it would lead to, and so it was a good thing there was no lifeguard about.

There's only one black spot on the horizon. Every time I look out of the patio doors I can see bloody Maxwell Grant. He's not doing anything, just standing there with his back to me. Sometimes he turns around and gives me a wave; it unnerves me, but he never comes anywhere near the house. Kay doesn't see him, which is just as well I suppose.

This place does need young people though, and we're looking forward to when Ethan and Denise return. We'll have a party for them and liven things up a bit. Kay frets about them, but they've got a good head on their shoulders and I know our son will phone if he's in trouble. No news is good news so they say.

As spring turns slowly into early summer, we enjoy sitting outside on the patio with a glass of wine in the evenings. I turn my back on Max, and look at my wife instead.

"Happy?"

"Of course." She replies. "Who wouldn't be?"

I take a sip of wine and survey the grounds. Kay's summerhouse is nearly finished, and the new lawn has taken very well. I've bought myself one of those sit-upon mowers, as I don't suppose Max will do much of a job unless he can move away from the wall. It's quite therapeutic to ride up and down and leave a lovely striped lawn at the end of the day. I even tried to run Max over as he waved to me, but the mower went straight through him and out the other side. It's rather eerie because when you're up real close to him and he looks at you, you find out that actually he's not really seeing *you*, he's looking at something else that's not in your line of vision.

The sun sets on another perfect day. Kay finishes her drink and hops over to sit on my lap.

"Am I getting heavy?" She asks. "I think I'm putting on weight."

I kiss her cheek.

"You look fine to me. Sit here much longer and we'll see what comes up."

Kay laughs.

"Oh no, not *that*!"

"I can't help it." I hold her closer. "You've got a lovely body."

"Shall we discuss my body further in the privacy of our bedroom?"

I give her an evil grin.

"There's nobody around. Why not discuss it here?"

I lay back on the sun lounger and laughing, she climbs on top of me. As I prepare for a pleasurable half hour, I quickly arrive at the conclusion that moving to the Hall is the best thing that's ever happened to us.

***

Kay sleeps soundly by my side. I lie perfectly content in our bed and listen to the house creaking as all the pipes settle down for the night, making a mental note as I lie there to ask the builders whether the central heating system is lagged properly.

For some reason I cannot drop off to sleep; I'm wired after our horizontal jogging session. Quietly I slip out of bed, climb into my pyjama bottoms, and open the bedroom door.

Emily stands there, pale and ethereal in that beautiful blue velvet gown that I remember so well.

At first I'm too dumbstruck to speak, and just stand there with my mouth open. Then the words come.

"You still don't look a day over twenty five."

She smiles and holds out one hand.

"That's because I *am* twenty five, John. It's the age I want to be."

I close the bedroom door behind me so as not to wake Kay. Emily wastes no more time on pleasantries.

"There are four men who at the moment are climbing over your gate. They have evil on their minds, and I am here to warn you. This is not my house anymore and I do not reside in it, but you *are* the father of my children. I cannot let you and your wife perish in the fire that they intend to cause."

The synapses in my brain are suddenly firing in all directions. I run to the window and peep around Percy's curtain. Sure enough, two hooded figures in dark clothing are on my driveway and helping a third one, a bit portlier, over the ten foot gate. I grab the nearest phone and dial 999. I look back over my shoulder to thank Emily, but she is nowhere in sight.

"Ambulance, police or fire brigade?"

"Police. Please send the police to Southcombe Hall, Church Lane, Southcombe. There are four intruders trying to gain entry. Hurry!"

I run back to the window. All four are now over the gate and creeping towards the house. I can see they're carrying what might be cans of petrol.

My heart hammers away in my chest; all thoughts of sleep forgotten. I rush downstairs to the fire control panel and slam my fist on the red button. There's no letter box for them to put a lit petrol-soaked rag through, but the oak door can only hold out for so long.

Smoke starts to filter through the bottom of the door. I run back upstairs and shake Kay awake.

"Come on!" I shout. "We've got to get out!"

She sits up, disorientated.

"Why?"

"Just put some clothes on and come downstairs!"

I can hear the sirens. Thank goodness there's a fire station in Southcombe. The police I hope are not far behind. I dash back down to the control panel and press the black button to open the gate. I hope the fire engines haven't driven straight through it and smashed it to smithereens.

***

Four miserable-looking youths, each cuffed to a police officer, regard me with malice. Kay and I stand on the driveway in our night clothes, while the fire brigade extinguish the last of the fires. Not much damage is done, except to the futures of Kelvin, Jayden, Tyler and Wayne.

It's a cool evening, and Kay shivers. I put an arm around her shoulders.

"Not much longer. I think the fires are out now."

"We'll have to get a restraining order on them." Kay replies. "They've obviously got it in for you."

"The judicial system will restrain them, hopefully."

I stare the youths out.

"We'll be back." Kelvin states half-heartedly.

One of the police officers starts to move Kelvin towards a squad car.

"Not if I've got anything to do with it."

My extra cheques weren't enough for them. I'm angry, and it occurs to me that I'll have to spend even more money now and get a shit-hot burglar alarm system installed. Living in sleepy old Southcombe where nothing ever happens isn't going to be such a bundle of fun as I'd first thought. I wish I'd never clapped eyes on the bastards.

CHAPTER 43 – EPILOGUE
JOHN

Emily, so far, has never returned since the night of the fire, and neither have I seen Robbie or Mia. However, I now think of Emily as a kind of guardian angel watching over me, as she certainly saved the house from major structural damage and us from being burned alive in our beds. I send out a silent prayer of thanks every night to wherever she might be. I also tend her grave, and stop the moss and weeks from taking over.

Kelvin and his friends are now back in prison, but I hear from the police that they're taking English exams and trying to better themselves. The police will let me know when all four are released, but somehow I'd like to hope that our paths will not cross again. There's an awesome burglar alarm system in the house now though; perhaps I was just a wee bit too naïve to think that nothing ever happens in Southcombe.

Ethan and Denise will return to the UK in July. We speak to them on Skype quite regularly, and they're more in love than ever. They'll both be heading off to University in October, and so whether their romance will last the trials and tribulations of separation is another matter. Ethan's going off to Durham to study Psychology, and

Denise has a teacher's course at Homerton, Cambridge. She's a nice girl, and Kay has already told her that she can stay with Ethan at our house in the holidays if her parents are away.

Kay has forgiven me for my love affair with Emily and for having the rectory burned down, incurring the wrath of the four Neanderthals. The two of us get along very well, rattling round our mansion. My head is clear enough to write again, and I'm halfway through what I consider is a terrific screenplay. I'm going to call it *For the Love of Emily'*…there's this ghost that appears as my main character sits minding his own business in his study…

Max still waves at me as he prunes his invisible tree. He's harmless enough, and I'm used to him now. I often wave back. I think I'm going to miss him when he eventually decides to head off to that celestial garden.

THE END

OTHER BOOKS BY
STEVIE TURNER

THE PILATES CLASS
A HOUSE WITHOUT WINDOWS
FOR THE SAKE OF A CHILD
LILY: A SHORT STORY
NO SEX PLEASE, I'M MENOPAUSAL!
A RATHER UNUSUAL ROMANCE
THE DAUGHTER-IN-LAW SYNDROME
REVENGE
THE NOISE EFFECT
CRUISING DANGER
THE DONOR
REPENT AT LEISURE
LIFE: 18 SHORT STORIES
ALYS IN HUNGERLAND
MIND GAMES
LEG-LESS AND CHALAZA
A MARRIAGE OF CONVENIENCE

If you have enjoyed this book, you may also like another paranormal story by Stevie Turner – *'Lily: A Short Story'*.

Lily is 92 and failing in health. Her family told her she was going on a little holiday, and although she finds herself still on her beloved Isle of Wight, to her horror she is now living permanently in a residential home at the mercy of Bridie, the 'horrible' one.

To make what is left of her life happier she thinks about years gone by, and once again wonders about the strange disappearance of her 14 year old sister Violet in 1897. Her depression lifts when another new resident manages to shed some light on the 76 year old mystery......

Review of 'Lily: A Short Story':

"One of the best books I've read all year. Lily—a beautiful person who suffered many tragedies in her lifetime. The writer had the uncanny knack of putting a reader right in the middle of the story. I felt so close to them. The ending is one of the most beautiful and moving finishes I have ever encountered. If I had to label it, I'd say that it was soulful. I know it left quite an impact on me. Excellent! "– *Carole McKee*